HAUN
WORLD

"On Epidoris," said Kennedy to his chief scientific advisor, "they have a strongly paternalistic system of government and there is evidence of rigid superstition. They believe in ghosts."

"Which makes the natives fit into the usual primitive culture," mused Luden. "The belief in ghosts is universal among races which have the imagination to form the concept of life after death. Is that what we are to investigate?

"No," said Kennedy. "We have to find out what happened to cause fifty-two men and a barracks to completely vanish."

THE
GHOSTS
OF EPIDORIS

by
Gregory Kern

DAW BOOKS, INC.
DONALD A. WOLLHEIM, PUBLISHER

1301 Avenue of the Americas
New York, N. Y.   10019

Cover art by Jack Gaughan.

*Dedicated to Ron Fortier,
Kennedy fan par excellence.*

FIRST PRINTING, FEBRUARY 1975

1 2 3 4 5 6 7 8 9

PRINTED IN U.S.A.

Chapter One

Lieutenant Charles Vickers woke up gasping, muscles jerking from the fading memory of a nightmare. Things had come to gibber as he hung suspended over an open flame. Faces had blurred into spined encrustations, mouths wreathed with tentacles; appendages had borne pointed scraps of chitin as sharp-edged and as hard as tough surgical steel. It was a bad time and he was well out of it.

Glancing at the luminous dial of his watch, he saw that there were still four hours to duty-time. It was too long a time to lie wakeful and too short to take a pill. Rising, he snapped on the lights, a delicate moonglow illuminating the small compartment which held his bed, a table and chairs, a cabinet and little else. A shower was attached and he stepped into the cubicle, setting the control for a hot blast followed by an ice-cold spray. Shivering, his skin goose-pimpling, he hit the hot-air button and relaxed as the created wind dried and warmed his flesh.

He dressed carefully, checking the insignia before putting on the green, blue and silver uniform. A new-made officer, he was proud of the silver bar, prouder still of the crest which held the figure nine. Commander Avery was a good man; only the best could hope to rise in the MALACA which was his responsibility.

Again Vickers checked his watch. Three hours still to kill.

A narrow passage ran past the door of his compartment, Kell lights strung at intervals along the roof. The cold blue light showed other doors to either side and opposite, all closed, each compartment holding a sleeping man. He walked softly to the end of the corridor where a stairway led to the level below.

At a desk the watch-officer looked up in surprise. "Up early, Charles?"

"Couldn't sleep. I had one hell of a nightmare."

"About girls you couldn't get?"

"No, about things that were getting me."

Lieutenant Ormond smiled. He was old and grizzled, outranking Vickers by virtue of seniority, but he had come late to his officer's insignia.

"It happens," he said. "I remember after we'd cleared up some trouble on Ecari I couldn't get to sleep for a week. Every time I closed my eyes I could see what the Elemquile had done to one of our patrols. Maybe you got it in indoctrination?"

"I did." Vickers was grim. "Flayed and set out in the sun. Eyelids removed and paste smeared over the raw flesh to attract sand-lice. And you were there?"

"I found them," said Ormond grimly. "We hadn't a hope in hell of getting them back alive—those that were still alive, that is." He looked at his hands. "I was senior non-com—our officer had been killed on the way into the hills. I had to make a decision and make it fast."

"And?"

"I killed them." Ormond's voice was harsh. "I burned the poor devils with a Dione. It was all I could do, as the inquiry agreed. That's why I couldn't sleep."

And that was how he had earned his commission, Vickers knew. The man had recognized the situation and had done what was necessary. He had later found the hive of the Elemquile to take a bitter revenge.

Vickers said enviously, "At least you were in action, Brad. It was tough, I know, but you had real work to do."

"Work I could have done without." Ormond leaned back, understanding. "You're young still, Charles, and impatient. It's natural, I guess. We all feel the same way at first—get in and clear up the mess and stop pussyfooting around. But it doesn't work out that way. Most of the time a MALACA is just hanging around in space, waiting and watching. That's why I'm glad of something like this." His head jerked toward a wall, the planet outside. "It breaks the monotony."

Vickers grunted, knowing the truth of what the older man said, yet not liking it. Crossing to the window, he activated the shutter and, as the metal slid upward, stared outside.

Epidoris was a bleak world. By daylight, when pierced by the savage glare of the tiny white primary, the deserts and hills showed sere and harsh and the looming mountains held a sense of dread. Even the leaden ocean was a sullenly heaving mass of gray water. At night, when the stars could be seen, the scenery took on a strangely disturbing appearance, as if things moved just beyond the edge of vision, freezing when directly looked at, moving again as the eye drifted on.

But at darktime, when the great ball of the binary system's dark star occluded the white dwarf, then the very air held mystery.

"Ghosts," said Ormond from where he sat. "That's what's out there now. Things long dead, resurrected to walk again, stalking the ground and jealous of those who now own what they once held."

"Legends."

"Maybe, but they are real enough for the natives. Not one of them ever ventures out at darktime. You know what their most severe form of punishment is? To be thrown outside at a time like this, to wander alone and unprotected among the ghosts."

"Nonsense," said Vickers without turning. "I know they do it, but it's still nonsense. A childish superstition. There's nothing out there but darkness."

"You could be right." Ormond, older and with more experience of alien worlds, was less certain. "But none of those who are thrown out are ever seen again."

"They could have got lost or been attacked by some predator."

"Which only comes out at darktime?" Ormond

shrugged. "You could be right about it all being superstition, but you'll never convince them of that. And, to be frank, I wouldn't be too eager to go wandering at a time like this myself."

Not that he would have to—the interdict was plain. At darktime all personnel were confined to stations and quarters. It was courtesy to the local government, perhaps, but the rule was enforced by military discipline.

Vickers looked to where the dark star hung almost directly above. The surface held a dull crimson light, giving the appearance of a smoldering wood fire thickly coated with ash. Around it shone a halo, a gleaming corona cast by its brilliant twin.

And darktime was not really dark. A host of stars threw a pale, nacreous luminescence over the distant town, the nearby bulk of grounded units, the tower and administration block, the assembled machines and other barracks.

A bustling hive of activity by day and normal night, the station was now a scene of desolation.

Looking at it, Vickers whispered:

"A savage place! as holy and enchanted
As e'er beneath a waning moon was haunted
By woman wailing for her demon-lover!"

"Samuel Taylor Coleridge," said Ormond. He had risen and now stood beside Vickers at the window. Quietly he continued:

"And from this chasm, with ceaseless turmoil seething,
As if this earth in fast thick pants were breathing,
A mighty fountain momently was forced;
Amid whose swift half-intermitted burst
Huge fragments vaulted like rebounding hail,
Or chaffy grain beneath . . ."

He broke off, shaking his head. " 'Kubla Khan,' " he said. "When he wrote it Coleridge must have had a vision of this place and what we're here to do. A great poet. You fond of poetry, Charles?"

"Some I like, some I don't." Vickers drew in his breath and turned from the window. "But a scene like that out there gets you. It has a strange kind of beauty. I'd like to go outside and walk around for a while just to get the feel of it."

"And then write a poem?" Ormond lifted his hand and touched the control, sending the window-shutter falling with a soft rasp of oiled metal. "Umbillia Obonga did that. He used to leave camp and go for long walks and then sit for hours, not talking, not even seeing, just thinking."

"You know Obonga?"

"I knew him," corrected Ormond. "He was in my squad way back. He'd have made a good soldier, too, but he decided otherwise. So he left the service."

And he became the most noted poet on seven worlds. Vickers looked at his fellow officer with enhanced respect.

"That man he wrote about in 'Paean for a Person.' You?"

"Us." Ormond was curt. "The squad. He took pieces from all of us."

"Was he with you on Ecari?"

"He may have been. I forget." Ormond added brusquely, "Forget it, Charles. Obonga tended to exaggerate."

Vickers nodded, knowing better than to press. He looked at his watch—still more than ninety minutes to go.

"You want me to take over, Brad?"

"Hell, no. What'll I do with the saved time? Look at walls?" Ormond riffled some papers. "Anyway, I've got to finish up these returns."

"I can do those."

"You could, but you're not going to. Make me the same offer some other time and I'll leap at it, but not now. Darktime's going to last a while yet. After reveille you can get the men to work checking their gear and doing the usual ship-drills. Now I'm in charge and what I say goes."

Vickers shrugged. "As you say, Brad, you're the boss. I'll have them double-timing right outside your door."

"Do that and I'll break both your arms." Ormond plumped into his chair, smiling. "And don't think I couldn't do it. You young sprouts sometimes need to be taught a lesson."

"Yes, daddy."

"And don't get smart, either." Ormond grunted as he moved a paper and a small package fell to the floor. "Hell, I forgot all about this. A runner brought this from the town for you, Charles. You were in the sack and he had to make time back. From the way he took off I'd guess that he made it." He threw over the package. "This another from that wonder-girl?"

"What makes you ask that?"

"It looks like a recording to me."

"So?"

Ormond shrugged. "Don't get so touchy, man. It's none of my business what you do off the job. I was just making talk." He glanced at his watch. "If you want to listen to it, go ahead. You've got plenty of time."

"Thanks," said Vickers. "I will."

Back in his room he closed the door and, from his box, took a player. It already held four disks like the one he had taken from the package, each four inches in diameter and an eighth of an inch thick. Slipping the new one on the spindle, he tripped the release and watched as it fell to the deck. A light pulsed and suddenly the area immediately above it became suffused with light. The rosy glow spread to form an area two feet across, a three-dimensional screen in which something moved—a woman, dancing.

She was tall and long-boned, with hips and thighs merging into a narrow waist which rose to spread into rounded shoulders and slender arms. She wore loose, diaphanous garments, scarlet fabrics which accentuated the whiteness of her skin, the supple grace of her body. Her breasts were high, full and proud, her neck a grace-

ful column of alabaster. Her feet were bare, ankles
ringed with tiny bells. There were more bells on her
wrists and others set in rings which adorned her tapering
fingers.

The bells made a thin, high-pitched ringing, shrill,
penetrating, filling the air with a chiming tintinnabulation, accentuating the throbbing beat of Heddish drums
pulsing a Kasedian rhythm.

The figure moved closer and became larger, small feet
drifting over a floor of polished stone, gilded nails catching the light and reflecting it, winking like the eyes of
serpents.

Crouching, eyes holding the rosy glow of the screen,
Vickers adjusted the volume, his senses quivering to the
drums, the bells. The other recordings had never been
like this. Now the girl was dancing with wild abandon,
her supple figure moving into suggestive postures, each
flowing into another even more open, more inviting. Her
dance was as old as time, a naked invitation, a promise,
a demand.

Women had danced like this before the ancient altars
of their gods in times long ago: writhing in front of the
sacred flames which spelled life to their communities,
dancing on the bare and naked ground at the end of
winter to insure the fertility which alone could prevent
starvation. The old, primitive symbolic magic which had
once ruled superstitious minds had never wholly been
forgotten.

Unconsciously Vickers began to respond, his hands
moving in time to the insidious rhythm, lifting, falling,
lifting again, as if he too were beating the taut skin of
drums, the very dirt itself. His lips parted a little as
he leaned forward from his squatting position on the
floor, his eyes fastened to the writhing body, the exqui-
site beauty of the face.

Her face was delicate, with skin drawn over prominent bone, the cheeks concave, accentuating the high
cheekbones, the elfin line of the jaw. The mouth was
full, the lower lip pouting a little, the teeth regular and
dazzlingly white. The forehead was high, rising to the

cascade of thick and richly ebon hair which hung like a waterfall of oiled jet over the smoothly sloping shoulders. The eyes were slanted elongations, abnormally wide, the irises lambent pools of violet.

This woman, this girl, was the epitome of female grace . . . dancing for him alone.

Dancing . . . bells ringing . . . vibrations built up to create harmonics which echoed from the walls, the roof. Amplified sounds met to augment each other as, unconsciously, he increased the volume . . . higher, higher until the stop had been reached and all the universe seemed to be filled with the pervading rhythm.

"Hey, in there!" Ormond's hand was at the door, his closed fist hammering. "You gone crazy, Charles? Cut out that noise!"

Vickers made no response, remaining before the player, deaf to everything but the sound, the shrilling, pervading sound.

"What's going on?" a deep voice called, thick with broken sleep.

"The walls!" Another. "They're quivering!"

"Vickers!" Ormond's shout was an angry roar. "Open up, man! That's an order!"

Sound welled up from the player, a peculiar combination of notes which now seemed to have a life of its own, a thing divorced from the mechanism from which it stemmed. It muffled the hammering, the snap of metal as the latch yielded, Ormond's boots as they carried him into the compartment.

Only when the other's big hand gripped his shoulder did Vickers stir.

"What's the matter?" He rose, face red with anger. "What goes on here? You've no damned right to come breaking in here like this!"

"Turn that thing off!" yelled Ormond. "The noise is—" He broke off as the dancing figure swirled, garments lifting, settling as she seemed to collapse to the floor, scarlet and gold making a flower-pattern about her figure.

The sound died except for a sympathetic humming

from vibrating metal as, on the player, an arm moved to sweep the recording from its place in order to make room for another.

The disk glided sideways, met the chute and hesitated for a fraction of a second before it slid down to lie beside the others.

As it touched, a gush of vivid yellow light burst from it and the other recordings. An expanding bubble of radiance touched the two officers, passed them, moved on into the passage, the walls. The sphere vanished almost as quickly as seen.

"What the hell was that?" Ormond blinked. "Did you see it?"

"It came from the player." Vickers gestured toward it, his hand freezing in mid-air. "Brad! What happened?"

The machine was ruined, a heap of plastic and metal slag from which a savage heat radiated.

"A booby trap." Old with experience, Ormond was quick to guess at an answer. "That recording must have been booby-trapped in some way. Set to explode when played."

"It didn't." Vickers, still dazed by the music, the dance, lifted a hand to run it through his hair. "The recording was over. It was being moved—no, it had been moved from the table when it happened. I saw it."

"Means nothing," snapped Ormond. "It could have been badly fused or the sonic trip may have slipped a little. My guess is that it should have blown when you were watching it. If I hadn't come in you could be dead now."

"No, the explosion—"

"Probably never happened." Ormond was impatient. "Or it may have been time-set to go off in your hands. Body heat alone would have done it once it had been primed. You didn't touch it, so it self-destructed. Damn it, man, can't you see what must have happened? Someone wanted to kill you and sent that recording to do it. If I hadn't come in and made you stand up you could have been blind by now or crazy."

"No. The girl—"

"To hell with the girl! This has to be reported." Ormond snapped an order to a face showing through the gap of a half-opened door. "You there! Take up post outside this room. No one to enter or leave without my say-so. Move!"

To Vickers he said, "Let's go and make our report."

The phone was dead. Twice Ormond punched the buttons, scowling as the screen remained lifeless. After the emergency switch had failed to produce an answer he slammed down the handset.

"This is where I get canned for breaking regulations," he said. "I'll have to break the interdict and make a personal report."

"Can't it wait?"

"No." Ormond glared his irritation. "You're still thinking of the girl," he accused. "Well, forget her. She has to be implicated in this somehow. The thing now is to make sure no one else plays one of those recordings. Try the phone again. If it doesn't work, I'm heading outside."

He crossed to the door, unlocked it, paused with his big hand on the knob. When Vickers shook his head he jerked it open.

And froze.

"What—" He turned, his face strained. "Vickers, get over here. Fast!"

He pointed outside as the other officer joined him.

"Tell me what you see out there. Quickly, man, tell me!"

There was nothing.

The grounded units, the tower, the assembled machines, the administration block, the other barracks—all had vanished.

Even the humped buildings of the distant town were nowhere to be seen.

Chapter Two

Beneath the runners the sand made a sibilant susurration, a dry rustling as of windblown leaves or a hand passed over raw silk, flesh against fabric generating tiny crackles of static electricity. Above, the sail strained at the mast, bulging, wood creaking, shrouds humming like vibrating strings.

At the tiller Kennedy could feel the frail shell of the sand-yacht quiver in response, each tiny lift of the runners sending its own message. The wind caught at his hair, pressed hard against his shoulders, sent streamers of the fine, powdery grit flying alongside, wreaths of sand as fine as smoke.

"Cap! We're winning!"

The girl at his side was young, her round face with the sparkling blue eyes thickly freckled. The suit she wore was vivid blue touched with crimson—a color combination matched in broad stripes on the sails and the pennon standing almost rigid above.

Behind and to each side, other yachts raced across the sands of Okeng, sails and painted hulls making bright patches against the rolling ocher plain.

"Bharch is getting close, Cap," she warned. "He could foul us at the turn."

"Better get down, Gwen," he warned.

"Not yet."

She rose to stand on tiptoe, one hand gripping a shroud as she leaned out over the hull. The wind sent her long blonde hair streaming past her face, the ends whipping. A hidden rock caught a runner and the craft

jerked, lifting to slew, sand pluming from the skids.
Only Kennedy's hand, reaching out, the fingers closing
like iron on her wrist, pulling her back and down, saved
the girl from being thrown from the yacht.

"Thanks, Cap," she said, rubbing her bruised flesh.
"Watch out for Bharch. He'll cut close behind us and try
to steal our wind. He might even veer ahead and force
us to yaw. This is one match he doesn't intend to lose."

Kennedy could see the man, close now, teeth bared as
he urged every ounce of speed from his craft. His two-
man crew crouched, ready and waiting to repeat a favorite maneuver; it was legal enough in this race, but it
could leave an opponent's craft totally wrecked, the
crew hurt or dead.

"Cap!"

Kennedy had no need of the warning. As Bharch
swept toward them, sliding in close behind for his own
sail to block the wind from Kennedy's, Cap pressed on
the tiller, sending his yacht out and away. The other
passed on an inward curve toward the flag which sig-
naled the turn.

"He's beating us!" The girl's voice held sharp disap-
pointment. "Cap, you let him through!"

"We'll pass him," promised Kennedy. "Penza!"

A man rose from the foot of the mast—a giant, almost as broad as he was tall. Sunlight reflected from the
shaven ball of his skull which surmounted a thick neck
over massive shoulders. The product of a high-gravity
world, Saratov was a living machine of flesh, bone and
toughened muscle.

"Ready, Cap. Now?"

"When I give the word."

Kennedy looked ahead, judging time and distance.
The yachts behind could be ignored. Another with sails
bright with yellow and green was too far out and,
though level, presented no threat. Bharch's yacht was almost directly ahead, the sail of orange and puce taut
against the pressure of the wind, runners whining as the
craft swung out to take the turn. It was a precautionary
measure, one Bharch could afford to take now that he

was confident of success. Too sharp a turn and the off-side runners would lift too high, stability would be lost and the craft would topple, to end in a mass of splintered wood and ripped fabric.

But Kennedy knew that he had to take the risk, if he still hoped to win at all.

"Gwen. To the off-side. Move!"

She obeyed, wind pressing her suit against the firm lines of her body as she slipped lithely beneath the boom to crouch beside the giant.

For a moment longer Kennedy waited, edging toward Bharch's yacht, seeing the other craft begin to swing toward him, to foul him should he continue his present course. Kennedy still had a choice, either to swing out beyond the other craft or to drop sail, spill wind and come to a halt.

And then there was no choice at all.

"Penza! Now!"

Kennedy dragged on the tiller as Saratov lunged over the side. The side runners were carried on slender booms of curved wood, narrow and giving little purchase. As the yacht came into the turn the off-side one lifted, rising as Saratov pulled himself along the support, using his giant strength to hang on, his massive weight to counterbalance the lift.

As the yacht tilted, the girl added her own weight, lying sprawled half out of the hull.

Sand rasped as the runners whined, plumes of dust rising, swirling, filling the air with a mass of choking grit. The tiller jerked against Kennedy's hands, fighting like a living thing, held by the bunched muscles of arms and shoulders. The direction of the wind changed; shrouds flapped, tautening, one breaking with the crack of a whip. The boom swung and the sail filled with a dull report and then, slowly, the hull began to level.

"We made it!" yelled the girl. "Cap! We made it!"

Behind lay Bharch's yacht, ahead fluttered the flags of the winning line, but Kennedy had eyes for nothing but the giant. He crawled over the edge of the hull, his face a mask of sand.

"Penza?"

"I'm fine, Cap." The giant's laughter rolled over the drone of the wind. "Are we going to win?"

Kennedy looked up at the sail. It was split but it would hold, and the broken shroud could be compensated for. Three long tacks and they would be home.

"Yes, Penza," he said. "We're going to win."

Chemile was waiting at the finish line. He stepped from the crowd as the yacht came to rest, a tall, thin figure with eyes like tiny jewels set in the smooth ovoid of his face. His skin bore faint traces of vestigial scales and was covered with minute flecks of photosensitive tissue which gave him the ability to adopt the coloration of any background—a man-sized chameleon with a highly adaptable attribute. The defense mechanism had been developed as protection against the predators which roved his native world.

"Cap!"

"Something wrong, Veem?"

"A message from Weyburn. He wants you to contact him immediately."

"Jarl?"

"He's over at the library. I've left word for him to join us at the *Mordain*."

Kennedy nodded, his eyes thoughtful. The library would have been a natural magnet to Professor Jarl Luden, who had little time for physical sports, preferring to browse among old volumes and scrolls. He could leave them without causing comment, but Kennedy was in a different position.

"Cap!" Gwen came toward him, the trophy in her hands. "Isn't it wonderful! This is the first time I've won and now I can sit at the upper table during the banquet. Of course, you'll be my honored guest. I never could have done it without you." Her eyes moved to where Saratov stood beside Chemile. "And Penza, naturally. You made the finest crew a girl could ever hope to have."

It had been her yacht, and now it would be her glory.

Kennedy said, "You'll have to count me out, Gwen. Something's turned up."

She frowned a little, a child who sensed the spoiling of her triumph.

"But, Cap, you've got to be there! You can't leave me now!"

"A relative," he lied. "A sudden illness. You understand."

She was immediately contrite. "Cap, I'm sorry. I guess I was being very selfish. And," she added with naked candor, "more than a little disappointed. I was hoping that, well, you know, to the victor the spoils."

"You are the victor, Gwen."

"No, Cap, I'm not and we both know it. I could never have won but for you." Her eyes roved his face, his body, sensing the firm lines disguised beneath the suit he wore. Sighing, she said, "Cap, where am I ever going to find another man like you?"

"You'll find someone, Gwen."

"Maybe." Again her eyes searched his face as if she wanted to memorize every detail: the hard planes of his cheeks and jaw, the directness of his stare, the mouth which was now gentle but which she felt could become cruel. "Cap, if you ever decide to marry, give me first refusal. Yes?"

"I'll think about it."

"For how long?" She shrugged, smiling. "You're a dilettante, Cap, drifting around and enjoying yourself. Maybe one day you'll settle down, but not yet. Well, give me a kiss and we'll call it goodbye."

"A nice girl," rumbled Saratov as she turned and walked toward her admirers. "I liked the way she handled herself on the turn. Well, it looks as if our vacation is over. I wonder what Weyburn has lined up for us now?"

Luden was at the *Mordain* when they arrived. His face was thin and lined, with a mass of grayish hair sweeping back from a high forehead. His body was sparse, almost boyish. The clothing he wore, a blouse and pants touched with bright colors, more color in the sash around his waist, gave him a peculiarly flamboyant appearance.

"Cap," he said without preamble, "I discovered something most interesting in the library. The record of a journey made by a Captain Elgh Xapetta. He mentioned a planetoid he landed on which held suggestive ruins. A wall on which he states he saw the Zheltyana Seal. Veem's message arrived before I could correlate the information but I had a copy made and—"

"We'll have time to study it later, Jarl," interrupted Kennedy. Like Luden, he too was interested in any facts concerning the mystery of the Zheltyana, the race which had spread across the known galaxy in ages past, leaving only tantalizing fragments behind after they had somehow disappeared. "First we must talk to Weyburn."

The Director of Terran Control held the semblance of a brooding eagle, his nose like a beak, his heavy jowls and pouched eyes matching the deep-graven lines running from nose to mouth. The weight of worlds rested on his rounded shoulders.

He said from the screen, "Cap, this is an odd one, but you're close and I think you'd better look into it."

"Trouble, Elias?"

"Yes and no. A mystery, rather. Two officers and fifty men of MALACA Nine have vanished. Their barracks too. The whole kit and caboodle, simply gone."

"Vanished?"

"I know it sounds crazy, Cap, but it happened. Avery sent me word. He says he can handle it, but I'm not so sure. I smell something wrong about it." Weyburn unconsciously lifted a finger to the side of his nose. "An intuition, but it worries me. Epidoris is a small, peaceful world and, for once, we don't have to worry about other powers. It has absolutely no strategic importance. Not even the Chambodian Complex could be interested."

Kennedy said, "Doesn't that rather put it outside our field of operation?"

"Maybe, Cap," Weyburn agreed. "I'll admit that I

can't see the need of a Free Acting Terran Envoy to become involved but, as I said, I've got a feeling. Something could be very wrong and, if it is, I want it nipped
in the bud. Commander Avery might be able to handle
it, but there's too much he can't do. You can."

Kennedy could go in, penetrate, infiltrate, bribe and
persuade, even assassinate if the need arose. He could
do anything necessary to stamp out the flames of incipi-
ent war—the aim and reason of FATE, of which Kennedy was the foremost agent.

And Kennedy could guess the reason for Weyburn's
concern. On his own desk, as on the desk of every
MALACA commander, on the bulkhead of every vessel, were written seven words: *Eternal vigilance is the
price of liberty.* No one connected with the defense of
Earth and its allied planets in the Terran Sphere could
ever dare to forget those words, Weyburn least of all.

"What is the background?" Kennedy asked.

"Nothing special. Just a world that asked for our
help. Affiliated, of course, but as I said, of no real importance. I'll send you the information over the copier.
Do what you can, Cap. I'll let Avery know you're on
your way. Out."

As the screen died a sheaf of papers came from the
radio-copier attached to the instrument, sent across
light-years of space by the magic of ultra-radio. Kennedy collected them and paused at the galley where Chemile and Saratov stood beside the coffee percolator, en-
gaged in one of their usual arguments as to who could
make the best brew.

"Action, Veem," said Kennedy, ending the discussion. "Set course for Epidoris."

"Immediate departure, Cap?"

"Yes."

"Trouble?" Saratov beamed at the prospect of a fight.
"I'd better check the guns, Cap. We don't want them
jamming if they have to be used."

That was a remote possibility, with the engineer nursing them as he did everything else mechanical about the

vessel. To Saratov, nothing but absolute perfection was good enough for the *Mordain*.

Luden looked up from a mass of documents as Kennedy entered the laboratory. "As I suspected, Cap, the report of Captain Elgh Xapetta is new. The planetoid he mentions is within fifteen parsecs of the Zhomboid Zone and it is barely possible that, at one time, it may have formed a part of one of the planets which now make up the Zone itself. In which case it is highly probable that other fragments of those worlds may be found within a similar radius."

"Perhaps, Jarl."

"A search might turn up items of great importance," mused Luden. "A high reward might encourage free-traders and various investigatory bodies to maintain a watch in that area. Perhaps we could even make a search ourselves."

"When we have time, maybe."

"True, Cap, when—" Luden broke off, pursing his lips as the lamps flashed red, the signal for takeoff. "I see that we are on our way. To where?"

"Epidoris, Jarl. What do we know of it?"

Luden touched a control and a screen lit up with the splendor of space. Stars glowing in a mass of glittering points merged with the distant fuzz of nebulae, sheets and curtains of luminescence blotched by the dull clouds of interstellar dust.

The view was relayed by the monitor from the screens. Stars blurred to flicker into steadiness as the *Mordain* reached and passed the velocity of light.

A touch on another control and the scene altered, became the depiction of a stellar chart, stars and nebulae flowing toward the edge, vanishing as a selected area gained dominance.

"Epidoris," said Luden as the depiction froze. "The single planet of a binary system close to Kiffa Australis. A small white dwarf and a large dark star circling each other around a common center. Epidoris has a complex orbit but would experience frequent eclipses of the bright primary by its dark companion. You have the surface data?"

"Yes." Kennedy looked at the papers in his hand. "Mostly desert and hills, a few small mountains, one ocean, few islands, rainfall very low, agriculture sparse. There are also signs of excessive heat in bygone ages."

"Perhaps the sign of a primary going nova," mused Luden. "The presence of a white dwarf leads inevitably to that conclusion. Normally I would have expected any orbiting worlds to be vaporized, but the presence of the dark giant adds a complicating factor. Had it been in the right position it could have acted as a shield," he explained. "There would have been a time of naked exposure, of course, but the brunt of the radiation could have been avoided. An interesting situation."

"For those alive at the time, no doubt," said Kennedy dryly. "But if they did survive no trace remains. The native life is relatively late." He looked at the papers. "A species similar to that of the Kanyo. Humanoid, intensely punctilious, somewhat primitive. Not that they can be wholly blamed for that. There are few easily accessible minerals and little surplus to encourage the support of a technological establishment. They have a strongly paternalistic system of government and there is evidence of rigid superstition. They believe in ghosts."

"Ghosts?"

"That's right, Jarl." Kennedy quoted from the papers in his hand. " 'Those who have departed and who are jealous of those who now own what once they held.' Both the initial sociological teams and Commander Avery are clear on the subject."

"Which makes the natives fit into the usual primitive culture," mused Luden. "The belief in ghosts is universal among races which have the imagination to form the concept of life after death. Is that what we are to investigate?"

"No," said Kennedy. "We have to find out what happened to cause fifty-two men and a barracks to completely vanish."

Chapter Three

"It happened. Don't ask me how, Cap, but it did." Commander Avery was grim. "The whole damned thing. Men, equipment, the building itself, everything. One minute it was there, the next it wasn't."

"Do you mean that precisely, Commander?" asked Luden.

"Near enough, Jarl. The tower was maintaining a regular monitoring of the area. Standard procedure to guard against theft or the unauthorized movement of personnel. And we have to watch for the infiltration of natives, who might be curious or simply careless. The watch-officer heard the alarm and went to check. That's when he discovered the barracks had vanished."

Commander Avery was a big man with a hawk-face and eyes which were creased with a mesh of tiny lines, now narrowed in baffled anger. His boots made soft thudding noises as he paced his office in the mother ship of MALACA Nine:

"I can handle most things, Cap," he said. "A war, a construction job, an evacuation—you name it and it can be done. But this has me beat and I don't mind admitting it. Logically it simply couldn't have happened."

"But it did," reminded Kennedy. "You've searched the area?"

"For a hundred miles all around. I've had fliers take samples of sand and rock from a thousand places. All negative. No signs of disturbance, no residual contamination, nothing to show movement of any kind. I've

24

spent days eliminating all possibilities. Now it's up to you, Cap."

Luden said thoughtfully, "What about the actual area itself, Commander? Have tests been made?"

"As many as we can think of, Jarl. If the barracks had been volatilized by some unknown force there would have been residual traces. None were found. I've even had the sand sifted to a depth of three feet. Nothing. Not a fragment of metal, a scrap of debris, the slightest trace of any chemical inconsistency. If they had been burned, reduced, dissipated in some way, we'd have found something. We didn't. Those men and that building simply disappeared, Cap. It doesn't make sense."

"Not on the face of it," agreed Kennedy. "But there has to be an answer and we must find it. Who is in charge on Epidoris?"

"Major Rebner is handling the operation, but Captain Shaffeck is investigating the disappearance. A good man, Cap. He'll give you all the cooperation you need. If there's anything you want, just ask for it."

That was an unnecessary reminder—as a Free Acting Terran Envoy Kennedy had the authority to demand the full use of every man and machine. He could even take over complete command if he felt it essential, but it was a power he never flaunted. Assistance, given willingly, was always better than aid forcibly obtained.

As the *Mordain* drifted from the lock of the huge vessel with Chemile setting course for the planet below, Luden said, "An intriguing mystery, Cap, and one which seems to be blinding Avery to the obvious."

"Which is, Jarl?"

"Only one of the barracks vanished. If due to natural causes of some kind I would have expected more than one to have disappeared. The local conditions were the same for all."

"So there has to be a human agency at work," said Kennedy. "A directed effort of some kind. But what would be the point, Jarl? The barracks was just a building and the men would be an encumbrance to any thief.

If anyone had wanted to sabotage the operation they would have turned their powers, whatever they are, against the equipment. Assuming, of course, that we are dealing with familiar motives."

"An assumption we have no right to make at this time, Cap," said Luden, thinly precise. "As yet we can only indulge in wild speculation which can serve no useful purpose. Right now I fail to see how any application of known forces could have achieved the results we are to investigate."

"Magic," rumbled Saratov from where he stood in the door of the laboratory. "Isn't that what you call the application of unknown forces, Jarl?"

"A primitive term, Penza, which provides a convenient answer to otherwise inexplicable phenomena." Luden was brittle. "And one which has no place in the vocabulary of anyone claiming to be a scientist. To use the word as an explanation is to use a nonsense-sound, one utterly devoid of meaning. Whatever happened must have a scientific explanation."

"I'll bet the natives wouldn't agree with you, Jarl," said Saratov, unruffled. "Any race which has a strong conviction of the existence of ghosts wouldn't hesitate to believe in magic."

"Ghosts!" snapped Luden. "More superstition. They, like magic, do not exist."

"Can you be certain of that, Jarl?"

"Yes." Luden was positive. "The day you make me a ghost-detector then I will give you credence to the actuality of such phenomena. And when you do we shall undoubtedly find that the things registered are due to natural causes, perhaps wild force fields of some kind. In any case there will be a logical, scientific explanation."

"Naturally," agreed the giant blandly. "Everything does once you know what it is. . . . When you don't, you call it magic."

"Really, Penza!" Luden's voice was acid. "I know that it amuses you to play the Devil's Advocate at times, but when you conduct such a discussion it gives me cause to doubt your—"

"How about some coffee, Penza," said Kennedy hastily. Good-natured banter was normal on the *Mordain* and usually he had to act as peacemaker. "One of your special brews. We've got time to enjoy it before meeting Captain Shaffeck."

Shaffeck was a short, thick man with a crop of red hair and sparkling blue eyes—an officer who seemed to radiate an aura of bustling energy.

"Cap! Jarl!" His grip was firm as he shook hands. "You wouldn't remember me, but I was signal-officer back when you had that trouble with Merah. You know what we're doing here?"

"Tell us," said Kennedy. He knew, but there were ways to gain cooperation and, talking, Shaffeck would relax. "A power installation, isn't it?"

"That's right." Shaffeck led the way across the upper room of the administration block to where a map and schematics hung against a wall. "We're running a couple of shafts through the planetary crust into the magma. Not into the liquid core, of course, but far enough down to obtain a high temperature. A chamber will be blasted at the nexus with remote-controlled atomics—I won't bore you with the specifications—and that's about all. See?" His finger touched the surface of the map. "One shaft will run back to here, where we are gouging a condensing system in the rock of the mountains. The other connects to the ocean. We've filled sluice gates and when everything is ready we'll complete the blasting of the channel. Open the gates and water will pour into the chamber, be converted into steam and try to escape. The inflow will block it so it will have to stream through the other shaft, past turbines and on to the condensing system. The result will be an endless supply of cheap power."

"Neat," said Luden. "Wouldn't standard atomic plants have done as well?"

"To supply power, maybe," agreed Shaffeck. "But

we're dealing with a low-economy culture with practically no industry and a complete absence of technological staff. Also, they need more than power. This way we supply an installation which trained men can maintain together with a constant supply of distilled water for irrigation. That area there"—again his finger touched the map—"is way down below sea-level. Filled, it will make a lake which can be tapped, canals for cheap transport, drinking water, the works."

"And encourage rainful," said Luden. "The area is ideal for development. When will it be completed?"

Shaffeck shook his head, scowling. "That's the big question. If we could work around the clock as we should be doing I could give you a firm answer. But we have local customs to contend with. No one works during darktime."

"Which is when the dark star eclipses the bright primary?"

"That's right, Jarl. When that happens everything comes to a halt, and I mean everything. You can guess what that means when you're driving shafts. Delays, delays and more damned delays. Sometimes I wonder if we'll ever get through."

Kennedy said, "The local workers put down their tools. And you?"

"We do the same. Commander Avery's orders. He doesn't want to risk offending the natives and, to be fair, he's right. Without them we couldn't manage. It's all for their benefit and they seem to appreciate that, but their beliefs are stronger than their desire to break out of the rut they're in." Shaffeck ran his hand through his cropped hair. "And it's some belief. At darktime no one goes out. No one. They have tunnels which connect up their houses; we just have to close down and wait."

His voice echoed his resentment, the frustration he felt, and Kennedy could appreciate it. A Mobile Aid Laboratory and Construction Authority was designed primarily for the defense of Earth and the allied planets of the Terran Sphere. A planet requiring aid received only machines and men enough to operate in a supervisory capacity; the bulk of labor had to come from local sources.

He said quietly, "Tell me about the missing barracks."

"Yes, Cap, of course, that's why you're here, isn't it?" Without waiting for an answer the captain led the way to a monitoring panel. "We run a slow scan over the entire area every seventy-five seconds. That's long enough for movement to become obviously apparent and slow enough to avoid continuous alarms if there should be wind shifting debris. The bowl is mounted on the tower and covers the area for a couple of miles in each direction. Wide enough to cover the installation and tight enough to give sharp definition. Well, it happened, and when I've said that I've said it all. One scan everything was as it should be, the next and the barracks had vanished. Lieutenant Jelinek was watch-officer at the time. When the alarm sounded he made a check, rechecked, then called me."

"The alarm is automatic?"

"Yes, Cap. We fix a pattern in the computer when all is settled and any divergence trips the siren."

Such a neat, foolproof system would reveal the presence of any man or group of men crossing the area. It would reveal too any other unusual activity within the field of the scanner.

"Seventy-five seconds," said Luden. "A trained man could run almost half a mile in that time."

"Not over that sand, he couldn't." Shaffeck was positive. "And he certainly couldn't have carried that barracks with him."

"I wasn't suggesting that he could," said Luden thinly. "I was merely estimating time and distance. I agree with you: no man or group of men could have done it. But a flier? A transport apparatus of some kind?"

"They could have come in fast," admitted Shaffeck. "And if they'd timed it to hit after the scanner had just passed they would have had over a minute in which to work. But one minute to grapple the barracks, rise and leave, and get beyond range of the scanner?"

"It seems a remote possibility," said Kennedy. "What was the barracks like?"

"Like those others you see out there. A Mark-seven."

The building was designed to contain accommodations for fifty-two men, recreational facilities, a dining room, storage and recycling apparatus, waste-disposal systems—a box twenty feet high, twenty-five wide, almost two hundred long, and heavy with the weight of men, stores, equipment, the fabric itself.

"When the alarm sounded what did you do?" asked Kennedy. "After you were summoned, of course. Did you examine the site?"

"Yes."

"Immediately?"

"At once." Shaffeck was emphatic. "Darktime was on the wane, anyway, but I didn't worry about that. I had lights assembled and called a general alert. Not even a mouse could have left the area without my knowing it."

"And?"

"It's all in the report, Cap. Nothing. The barracks had simply vanished without a trace."

Luden said sharply. "Is that wholly true, Captain? I don't doubt that you believe what you say, but often what we see is not all that there is to be seen. There could be some trifle which you disregarded at the time as being unimportant. Now think, were you the first to reach the site?"

"One of the first. There were a couple of others with me, but none before."

"And the time-lapse?"

Shaffeck frowned, thinking. "I heard the alarm and then Jelinek called me. Call it half a minute. Say another two before I'd ordered the lights and a general alert. Add a little more until I got outside to make a personal examination of the area. Four minutes at the most. The place was, of course, under electronic surveillance at all times."

"And nothing was seen," said Kennedy. He knew

what Luden was driving at. "But the site itself, did you notice anything unusual about it?"

"The report—"

"To hell with the report!" snapped Kennedy. "You turned that in after you'd had time to think about things. I want your initial impressions."

"Such as?"

"If I told you I'd be feeding your mind. You went out, it was darkish, men had lights. You approached the spot and . . . ?"

"I halted," said Shaffeck. "There were a lot of shadows and I thought I saw something, but it must have been a trick of the light. A thing like an animal," he added hastily as he saw Kennedy's expression. "Something as large as a horse with crocodile jaws and a tail. It was just a glimpse. One thing, though, it was way above ground, as if it was standing on thin air."

"Did it move?"

"Not that I noticed. As I say, I only saw it for a split second—or thought I saw it. And there were no tracks, so it couldn't have been there at all, could it?"

"Why ask me?" said Kennedy. "Anything else?"

"No, I—" Shaffeck broke off, then said slowly, "Yes, now that I come to think of it there was. We were busy, you understand, and it didn't register at the time, but where the barracks had stood was a sort of rim—a ledge as if sand had been blown against it and had been left standing. There was a little wind, more gusts than anything else, and I guess they must have blown it down when I made a closer examination. I'd forgotten it, Cap. That's the truth."

"Anything else?"

"No. That's all. I'm certain of it."

"And have you any explanation, no matter how wild, as to what happened?"

"Explanation?" Shaffeck's laugh was brittle, humorless. "No, Cap. None to beat Myaz Sharn's."

Chapter Four

"Ghosts." Myaz Sharn spoke with the absolute conviction of a man who held no shadow of doubt. "I assure you, my dear Kennedy, that is the answer. The ghosts took your building and your men."

Kennedy said flatly, "That is not an answer which satisfies us, your Serenity. In our experience ghosts are intangible creatures of the imagination."

"Then you are fortunate indeed." Myaz Sharn leaned forward from where he sat in a decorated chair and picked up a fuming censer, inhaling the pungent smoke as it rose to wreathe about his narrow, wide-eyed face. "On Epidoris it is not so. Men have died proving it."

"Died?"

"They vanish. Would they have done so of their own desire? And a man who is no longer with his family and friends can truly be said to have died. Is that not so?"

Kennedy knew this was specious reasoning, but he did not make the mistake of saying so. The ruler was a product of his culture and to him, as to any of his people, the concept of anyone willingly leaving his family and tribe was unthinkable.

Myaz Sharn leaned back in his chair, inhaling, an old man, his skin creped with a mesh of lines, his skull sharply crested and tufted with silver hair. The ears were like those of a dog, peaked and uplifted. His body, muffled by ornate robes, was humped at the shoulders. His hands, wrinkled and sere, each bore six fingers.

"We are an old people," he mused through the smoke. "Legends tell us that we came in a metal egg from a place far away, guided by a beneficent spirit to this world which was barren of life. A vessel of space, of course, that much is now obvious, but the science we must once have owned was lost in the struggle to survive. Now, perhaps, it will be regained. Our young men, trained by your people, will cause the deserts to bloom. I shall not live to see it, but I will go to my rest happy that it will be done."

"And others? Are they as happy?"

"A few are not," admitted Myaz Sharn. "Those who have high places are always reluctant to see change. Some nobles would prefer your people to leave and allow us to go on in our own way. They are blinded by their own selfishness. They cannot see that customs must change and that all, not a few, must be given the chance to enjoy the rich harvest the future can bring. But they are old and will die, and their sons will be more amenable to what must be."

"Die," said Kennedy. "And turn into ghosts? To wander this world jealous of those who now own what once they held?"

"No." Myaz Sharn set down his censer. "Not they. When we die our spirits go to live on the dark sun."

"But the ghosts?"

"They are real. They belong to the ones who owned this planet in the past. But surely you know that?"

Kennedy frowned, realizing the mistake which had been made. To the sociological investigators ghosts meant only one thing: a superstition to be fitted into a familiar pattern and then ignored as being of no real importance. But to the natives the word could have a different connotation.

"These ghosts," he said. "Has anyone ever seen them?"

"Those who vanish, surely yes. Others?" Myaz Sharn paused, then continued slowly. "Once, when I was young, I went hunting in the hills. There are savage predators there, the descendants of domestic animals which have long run wild. It was growing late but I was eager to make a kill and would not listen to the warnings. As the prince I was obeyed. Darktime caught us in the open. It was an experience I never wish to repeat."

"You saw something?"

"Glimpses, no more, but they were enough. The guide was old and wise and knew what to do. He found a cave in which we huddled with the opening blocked by packs and the skin of the beast I had slain. In that we followed the example of the predators. Later, when I went to find the body of the dead creature, it was gone."

Perhaps it had been eaten by smaller, nocturnal creatures, Kennedy thought, but he didn't say so. A man lived by his faith and it was never wise to call a man a fool.

He said, "These people who are against the installation, would they be prepared to take strong measures against it?"

"No."

"With respect, your Serenity, can you be sure of that?"

"You think they would dare to defy me?" For a moment youthful fire glowed in the wide-set eyes. "For them even to consider it would be against all tradition and custom. And should they be so insane as to try, then they would be punished."

Kennedy noted a hint of barbaric ruthlessness, born, perhaps, in the days when each moment was a struggle to survive, now ingrained in the culture of the race. He looked past the ruler, to the walls of the chamber in which he sat, the mosaics, the paintings, the tapestries of faded material—relics of an age when men had walked armed and armored, touchy about their pride. They were still obsessed with an elaborate system of social codes, offense taken at the inflection of a word, a glance, but time and change would alter that.

Carefully he said, "About the installation, your Serenity. Now that the shafts have been opened it would be possible for men to work in them during darktime. They would be under cover and unexposed."

"And your own people?"

"We also. Arrangements can be made so that local customs are not offended. I make the suggestion, but I do not urge it. Should it be followed then progress will be accelerated."

"And the sooner the job is finished the sooner your people can leave?"

"That is so."

Again Myaz Sharn picked up the fuming censer, his face veiled with the rising smoke. He inhaled, enjoying the vapor, the scent of herbs and volatilized oils. He was an old man, brooding, calculating, taking his time to formulate a decision.

It was what Kennedy had expected.

"I must think about it. There are factors to be taken into account and other interests to be considered. Also, custom is against it."

"I understand, your Serenity."

"For a member of a young and boisterous race you are tolerant," said Myaz Sharn. "Impatience is a thing to be avoided at all times. Today, tomorrow, all things will be as they must. I am an old man, yet in my journey through life I have learned things of value: To be patient. To be humble. Never to make the mistake of thinking that, because I know a part, therefore I must know the whole. Danger awaits the unwary; the path is not always as firm as we may think. To travel slowly is, at times, to make the faster progress."

"Look before you leap," said Kennedy. "An old proverb of our people, your Serenity."

"And a good one. I think we understand each other." A gong murmured as Myaz Sharn touched it with his hand. "Be free to ask audience at any time."

An attendant, answering the summons, guided Kennedy from the palace, a building little higher than the others which formed the ancient city. Streets wound in apparent confusion, narrow, paved with blocks of stone. Doorways were arched and held thick doors which would be firmly closed during darktime. The windows held bars and could be shuttered from within.

Kennedy walked down a main street ranked with

shops selling a variety of goods. They were small, the windows cramped, the interiors redolent of spices, leather work, perfume, tisanes, fats and oils of a dozen kinds. One held electronic equipment, primitive transitor radios, players, recorders, the advance goods of the flood which would shortly arrive to herald the new technology. A sedan chair passed, carried by brawny runners, sweat gleaming on oiled skin. In the interior a veiled and ornamented woman lounged with idle grace, a relic of the past. Myaz Sharn would have to take these factors into account, as he would all the shops and businesses: the sellers of local goods which would serve as souvenirs, the taverns and places of entertainment, the cafés selling skewers of spiced meat, stews of pungent vegetables, blends of fish and fowl fried and served with paper-thin disks of baked dough set with crushed nuts and larded with syrup.

To the woman the arrival of Commander Avery's men would be a nuisance, a disruption of familiar ways. To the others the installation meant a stream of wealth from the crewmen and officers, additional business they would be reluctant to lose.

And others had arrived, vultures eager to join the feast, entrepreneurs willing to pay high fees for their concessions.

A girl, her body shapely in gaudy fabrics, her face painted in a psychedelic pattern, touched Kennedy's arm as he passed.

"Hi, handsome! Lonely?"

She was a Cissurian—a people noted for erotic skills and notorious for harpy-like greed—sent to wander the streets to advertise the dubious pleasures of the mobile emporium parked at the edge of the city.

Kennedy shook his head. "No."

"A pity." She could have been beautiful beneath the paint. She stared at him, her eyes bold, examining his face, the clothing he wore, nacreous material bearing an abstract design in delicate strands of gold. "We've got a full range of sensory tapes from Azor. Full stimulation. Cheap too, but I don't suppose that bothers you."

"You're wasting your time."

"It's mine to waste. How about it, handsome? A break from monotony. Music, wine, all you need. Good food too, and all at a low rate. Bring a friend and you get a bonus. A touch of home right on your doorstep. Ask for the Blue Bell."

Smiling, he shook his head.

"You could change your mind, handsome. If you do I'm Syrella. I'll be looking out for you."

Kennedy passed on, heading toward the parking lot and the jitney he had ridden in from the installation. A deep booming came from an open door, a musical throbbing interspersed and accompanied by a thin, undulating wail: the natural music of the lower classes of Epidoris, sounds made by trained throats and lungs.

From the interior of the tavern came a yell, the sound of cheering.

"I won! Pay up, Earthman!"

The room was small, the ceiling low, the light from the door and a few lanterns barely relieving the gloom. The musicians squatted on a raised dais, two men and a boy, booming and wailing, indifferent to the scene before them.

A heavy man sat at a table to one side, thick muscles showing beneath a torn shirt, metal gleaming in his ears, his nose flared, his mouth a gash. Thick hair grew low on a sloping forehead and his brows were tufted over deep-set eyes of muddy brown. Kennedy identified him as a Helgian, probably a bouncer or a fighter from one of the concessions.

Facing him, a brawny man wearing a MALACA uniform scowled as he nursed his right hand. Others, similarly dressed, stood around him, none looking cheerful.

"I won," said the Helgian again. "They all saw it. Pay up!" He grinned as money rattled on the table, piling up between smoking flames which stood at each side. "You want to try again? Any of you?" His eyes roved the crowd, a mixture of races, locals and those from the concessions. "You, then." He stared at the man who nursed his burned hand, a sergeant. "Want to try again? Win back what you've lost?"

"Go to hell!"

"Cowards, the lot of you," sneered the Helgian. "That's the trouble with you Earthmen. No guts. You can't take a beating. Get hurt a little and you run to hide in a hole." His eyes lifted to fasten on Kennedy. "How about you, pretty boy?"

Kennedy looked at the sergeant. "What's this all about?"

"Indian wrestling. I thought I was good at it, but now I'm not so sure. But I'd have won if he hadn't cheated. The swine kicked me under the table."

"My foot slipped." The Helgian shrugged. "Tell you what, tie my legs to the chair if you want. No? Well, it's as I said, gutless, the lot of you."

Kennedy said, "Never mind tying your legs, but if you kick me I'll tear out your throat. How much do you bet?"

He matched the coins and took his place facing the other, one elbow on the table, hand gripping the Helgian's. The palm was hot, thick with calluses, the fingers hard with muscle. To either side the flames guttered, waiting to be quenched by the loser's hand.

"Remember what I told you," said Kennedy. "Sergeant, give the word!"

He felt the pressure as it came, the abrupt surge with which his opponent hoped to end the contest, saw the muddy eyes blink as his own hand and arm held firm. For a long moment they remained locked in stasis and then Kennedy steadily fed power into his arm, tensing the muscles of biceps and shoulders, turning his forearm into a rigid bar of flesh and bone . . . a bar which swung relentlessly to one side, carrying the trapped hand with it, passing the point of no return. The low flame singed the mat of hair lowering toward it, seared the skin beneath, then died as Kennedy rammed the hand on the guttering fire.

"You cheated!" The Helgian was sweating. "I wasn't ready."

"You heard the signal." Kennedy scooped up the money he had wagered, gestured for the sergeant to take the rest. "Do you still think Earthmen are gutless?"

He heard the noise as he turned toward the door, the rasp of wood as the table was thrown aside, the yell of warning. He ducked, avoiding the chair which tore through the air where his head had been, the wood splintering as it smashed against a wall.

Turning, he met the rush of the Helgian.

The man was big, broad, fast on his feet. He dodged and crouched, adopting the stance of a boxer, his fists darting forward, feinting, his left hand aimed like a club at Kennedy's jaw.

It missed as Kennedy swayed to one side and then moved in, the stiffened edge of his right hand slamming like a blunted ax on the thick biceps, the rigid fingers of his left burying themselves deep into the rotund belly. Air gushed from the man's lips as he doubled, the numbed left arm hanging helpless at his side.

He should have quit then, but he was a fighter, mad with rage, and he still had one working arm and two feet.

He lunged forward, right arm lifted, fingers curved to claw at Kennedy's face and eyes, right boot swinging in a vicious kick.

Kennedy slammed aside the arm, caught the boot with his free hand and, stepping back, lifted the trapped foot and twisted it at the same time. Thrown off balance, the Helgian fell with a crash to lie, semi-stunned, on the soiled wood of the floor.

"Had enough?" Kennedy stared down at him, his face grim. "The next time you try that I'll break your leg. Now get the hell out of here before I change my mind."

As the man crawled away the sergeant said, "Mister, I'm going to buy you a drink. The best in the house. The way you handled that character was a treat for sore eyes. You working a concession?"

"No." Kennedy took the proffered glass, sipped and

tasted a blend of herbs and pungent fruits. "Why do you ask?"

"I was hoping you could give me an introduction to someone." The sergeant lowered his voice. "Someone special. She's an entertainer at the Ultima Thule. That's a high-class joint catering to the luxury trade, officers and such. I managed to get in—never mind how." His wink was expressive. "They had this girl and she's a dream. I managed to sneak a shot of her. I had the word and went prepared, borrowed one of the all-light cameras from the stores. See?" He produced a colored print. "They call her Zilma, Princess Zilma Narayan."

Taking the print, Kennedy said, "May I keep this?"

"Sure, I've got others. A peach, isn't she? A real dream. The kind of girl . . ."

He rambled on, but Kennedy wasn't listening. He stared at the photograph, at the remembered face, at the jewelry around the slender neck—a delicate filigree of gold fashioned in an elaborate design . . . the symbol of the double helix.

Chapter Five

"Kaifeng?" Saratov's boom echoed throughout the *Mordain*. "Cap! If that thing is still walking around alive I'll—" He broke off, his voice becoming puzzled. "But how can he be alive? We saw him die."

"No, Penza," corrected Luden. "We did not."

"But his base—"

"Was utterly destroyed, I agree, both by the interior explosion of his power supply and the impact of our own torpedoes. But we did not actually see Kaifeng himself destroyed."

"You're splitting hairs, Jarl," said Chemile. He stood with the others in the laboratory, looking at the print Kennedy had placed on the desk. "You don't actually have to see a bug squashed when you crush the nut it's in to know that it's dead. We cracked Kaifeng's nut, his base, and he must have gone with it. How could he have escaped? He was present, we know it, and that is that. Right, Cap?"

For answer Kennedy pointed at the photograph, at the symbol it contained.

"So it's a girl wearing a necklace," said Chemile. "One carrying the sign of a double helix. So what?"

"Kaifeng's insignia, Veem."

"Coincidence." Chemile looked from one to the other. "Listen," he said impatiently. "We saw what happened. The whole base, almost the entire planetoid was totally destroyed. We watched the whole time and no ship escaped. Kaifeng must be dead."

"We thought that once before," reminded Saratov.

41

"We were wrong then and we could be wrong now. I admit it's unlikely, but I suppose it is possible. Just barely possible."

"The first time we saw the flicker of his ship as it escaped," snapped Chemile. "We didn't know it at the time, but that's what it was. We didn't make the same mistake twice. Had we seen anything like a ship escaping from that planetoid we'd have been after it. We didn't, so one couldn't have existed."

Kennedy said slowly, "Not one that we saw, Veem. That doesn't mean there couldn't have been one."

"Cap?"

Kennedy remained silent, thinking, remembering. He had just escaped from the base and the *Mordain* was streaking into space to avoid anticipated missiles. They halted and turned to the attack with all systems alert. Then came the close watch for the expected blossom of released atomic fury, the internal destruction released by the slaves of Kaifeng.

"Cap?" Chemile was anxious. "I'm right, aren't I? He couldn't have escaped?"

"I think he could, Veem, and I'm afraid that he did. There were a few moments as we left the base when his ship could have left the lock and used the bulk of the planetoid to shield its escape. We know that it has fantastic velocity. A tunnel could even have been driven to the far end of the planetoid as an emergency escape route. The ship could have entered it, waited until we had left, then escaped."

"A remote possibility, Cap," said Luden. "And one which cannot be ignored. But I think it would be a mistake to assume too much. Aside from the device of the double helix there is nothing to form an association with Kaifeng. And, as Veem pointed out, the presence of the emblem could be due to sheer coincidence."

"The insignia maybe, Jarl. But the girl . . . I've seen her before."

. . . Resting in a casket deep in the secret base, newly grown, freshly awakened. She was a product of the warped genius which had assembled a group of able sci-

entists to manipulate the very basic matter of life itself
and adapt it to his whims. The girl was a threat to the
Pax Terra, and Kennedy had been convinced he had destroyed her. He had thought her incredible beauty was
dissolved in spreading waves of atomic fire.

"Cap, are you certain?" said Luden when Kennedy
had explained. "You only caught a glimpse of her, remember. And genetic characteristics can be repeated by
accident. This dancer—" He turned over the print and
read the name. "This Princess Zilma Narayan could
have certain similarities. The bone structure of the face,
for example, the eyes—as an entertainer they could be
artificially tinted and probably are."

Saratov rumbled, "I'm with Cap on this. How many
coincidences do you need before you can accept what is
before your face? The girl alone—a coincidence, maybe. The insignia—another, maybe. Put them together
and I smell a rat. That devil's alive and kicking somewhere, and I'd bet that he's close."

"But if the girl is the one Cap saw, then why brand
her with his emblem?" asked Chemile. "Is he begging to
be noticed?"

"No, Veem," said Luden. "The answer lies in his psy-
chological makeup. Kaifeng has a tremendous ego. He is
subconsciously driven to mark all that is his. It is, in a
sense, an extension of his personality. We already know
that he is consumed with ambition and seeks to own everything, literally. And remember how unlikely it would
be for anyone to make the association. Kaifeng wouldn't
know that Cap had ever seen the girl. It would be perfectly safe to display her, but the question which puzzles
me is why show her at all?"

"As bait," said Kennedy flatly.

"A lure, Cap?" Luden frowned. "But for what purpose? Kaifeng is devious, we know that, but I fail to see
any possible motive. It is still probable that the girl is in-
nocent and the necklace a coincidence."

"Perhaps." Kennedy picked up the photograph. "Penza, copy this and have prints shown to every officer. I
want to know if any of them has or ever had any asso-

ciation with her. Veem, ask Terran Control to check on the movements of a mobile emporium called Ultima Thule now on Epidoris. Jarl, we'd better see Major Rebner."

Rebner was a tall, gangling man with a lantern-jaw and deep-set eyes. He looked up from a communicator and nodded a greeting.

"A moment, Cap, I'm busy."

"Take your time, Major."

Another nod and Rebner was talking to a man two hundred miles away in the mountains. "You're falling behind on the condensing system, Boyd. Speed it up. Never mind the trimmings, just get the main galleries completed. What? The aural effects? I'll check. Yes, yes, I know, but don't tell me, just get it done." He pressed a button. "Cremsley? When are you ready to fuse? No good. It'll be darktime soon and we'll have to button down. I want that section completed. Yes, send out the natives and use remotes. Right."

Leaning back, he said, "Well, Cap, when can I have my men and barracks?"

"As soon as we find out where they are. Trouble with sound?"

"Sound?" Rebner frowned, then shrugged. "I get it, the aural effects I mentioned. Boyd's just remembered that the initial investigation made a point of us not producing too high-pitched a note. When the steam hits, those galleries are going to turn into a king-sized organ unless we take care. Deep sounds are acceptable, high ones are out. It's against their religion or something. We can fix it by cutting channels to create an opposed harmonic. No problem. Now, about those barracks?"

"I have run a series of tests," said Luden. "All negative as yet, but even negative information can be of value. In a way I am duplicating what has already been done but to my own satisfaction. I intend to continue the testing during darktime. I have your permission?"

"I can't refuse it," said Rebner bluntly. "But I wish you wouldn't. The natives are getting touchy and are slowing down. You heard what I was saying. That vanishing has upset them; there's been a lot of talk about the anger of the ghosts and such. If anyone else went missing it could almost shut down the operation."

"As bad as that?" Kennedy asked.

"I'm not exaggerating."

"I didn't think you were, but Myaz Sharn—"

"Sits in his chair and sucks in that smoke and lives in the past," interrupted Rebner. "Did he tell you of the faction that's against all this?" He gestured at the installation. "If so I'll bet he discounted it, right? Well, he's making a mistake. He thinks he can ride two horses, but he's going to wind up on his rear if he isn't careful. The old guard wants things as they were, and they are getting restive about the way things are going. The new guard wants change as fast and as complete as possible. They think that machine-style power equates with political-style power. They could be right."

"They are," said Luden. "Those who control the source of production also control the political arena."

"In theory," said Kennedy. "Not always in fact." He thought of the ruler, remembered the iron he had sensed in the man. He was old but not stupid, and he had asked for the installation to be built. "What you're saying, Major, is that the situation is delicate, a balance, if you like. If opinion veers a little too far then there could be trouble."

"Either revolution or a complete withdrawal of labor," agreed Rebner. "Either way we and the planet both lose. It's these damned ghosts! If they've taken to snatching our own men, how can we convince the natives that they don't exist?"

"The men and the building," reminded Luden.

"Which makes it worse, Jarl. Safety used to be assured if they stayed indoors. Now that a complete barracks has gone, how can they feel safe? And it's no good telling them that it's all a lot of superstition; they simply won't believe it." He stabbed at a button. "Arn? Get hold of Coro and send him up here."

"It's getting late, Major."

"I won't keep him long." Rebner released the button. "A native," he explained. "A foreman and a good one. He joined us at the beginning. Talk to him. You'll see what I mean."

The native was a typical product of his class, his shoulder-hump pronounced, eyes wide, skin dull from lack of oils. His ears twitched as he stood before them in his clean issue coveralls.

"You're afraid of darktime," said Luden. "I know it is because of the ghosts, but have you ever seen one?"

"Never, sir."

"Then how do you know they exist? People tell you, right? But have they ever seen a ghost?"

"No, I—" The man broke off, struggling to explain. "To see a ghost is bad," he continued. "It brings ill-fortune. Those who see them say nothing. Your men saw them and those men are gone."

"Who told you that our men saw them?" asked Kennedy.

"People. The word passes, as did the warning and the prophecy. I do not believe everything that is said, but others do. The ghosts must not be disturbed, they say. If aroused they will seek vengeance. They will grow stronger and take houses and those inside the houses. So it was foretold."

"By whom?" Kennedy's voice held the iron of command. "Answer me, Coro. Who told you all this?"

"People. Please, it is getting late."

"One last question. Do you honestly believe that what happened here was due to ghosts?"

"But of course, sir. What else?"

"Now you know why I'd rather you didn't work outside during darktime, Jarl," said Rebner as the native left the office, almost running in his eagerness to be on his way. "One more disappearance and we could be out of business."

Luden said stiffly, "Major, I refuse to give credence to local superstition. Ghosts simply do not exist."

"Maybe not, but if they do I'd rather one didn't get you."

"Really—"

"You can use remotes," said Kennedy, interrupting Luden's protest. "Instruments can be set up for initial testing and read by monitor. Better hurry if you want to get them going, Jarl. And we have to check on what Penza may have found."

It was little. Most of the officers had seen Zilma Narayan, but none had actually spoken to her. Many had recordings of her performances.

"One thing though, Cap," said the giant. "I did pick up a rumor. Lieutenant Vickers seemed to have a crush on her. He collected every recording available, four in all. He may even have spoken to her, but no one can be certain."

"Vickers," said Kennedy thoughtfully. "One of the officers in the barracks which vanished. Get one of those recordings, Penza. We'll play it in the *Mordain*."

The roseate cloud swelled to reveal a slim, heavily veiled figure standing on a row of drums. Small hollow gourds hung from her arms and wrists, and her bare feet glided over the taut skins. The beat was slow and solemn at first, then quickened to a pulsing thunder, catching and accelerating the beat of the heart. The tones were strangely muted, confined, rolling with whispering echoes through the vaults of ancient temples, throbbing with an aching yearning.

"Superb." Luden drew in his breath. The playing had held the touch of genius, the dancing a liquid grace. "Is that the girl you saw, Cap?"

"I'll know that after I've been to the Ultima Thule." Kennedy answered.

Chapter Six

It was late when they left, the orb of the dark sun almost touching its bright companion; darktime would begin shortly. Hunched in the seat of the jitney, Saratov brooded as he stared at the landscape, the bleak terrain. Parts of it—the rounded mountains, the sand, the sparse and stunted vegetation—reminded him of Droom, the planet of his birth. Even the roofs of the city-buildings held a strange familiarity, low and rounded, as suited to the drag of high gravity; soaring spires and graceful pinnacles would have been inappropriate.

Kennedy glanced at him as he handled the machine.

"Thinking of home, Penza?"

"Not really, Cap, just thinking. These people must lead a hell of a life, terrified as they are. Do you think we'll find Kaifeng?"

"If he's here, Penza, we'll find him." Kennedy was grim. "Check with Veem to see if he's got anything on the Ultima Thule."

Lifting his wrist, Saratov touched a stud on the communicator disguised as a watch, a twin to the one Kennedy wore.

"Veem? Anything come through yet?"

Chemile's voice came thinly from the instrument: "Nothing concrete. A mobile with the same name stayed for a while on Zadoc. No entertainer listed as Zilma Narayan. There isn't much hope of tracing it; most of these things change names at almost every planet they hit."

Kennedy said, "Owner?"

"On Zadoc it was a man calling himself Emil Groach,

48

a native of Lepash. They left clean, but there were complaints of customers having been cheated."

Kennedy had not expected much else. Dodging a rough patch in the road which led from the installation to the city he said, "Tell Veem to monitor, Penza. Just in case."

"So you do expect trouble, Cap," said the giant as he finished relaying the instruction. "I knew it. That's why I insisted on coming with you."

Kennedy slowed as they neared the parking lot, halting the vehicle, locking it as they left. The town was already empty, the streets deserted, a solitary window showing a patch of illumination. A shutter fell across it as they watched and the sonorous notes of a bell echoed from somewhere.

Kennedy glanced at the sky. The suns were touching. The curfew-warning ended as a first small segment was bitten from the tiny white sun.

Now, according to local legend, danger stalked the land and only a fool or a criminal would remain outdoors.

"We'd better hurry, Penza."

Kennedy led the way, his long legs eating the ground. Saratov kept at his side, wearing the loose robes which gave him the appearance of a normal man grown obscenely fat. The concession area lay to the north of the parking lot, great mobiles lying close to smaller installations, booths and stalls. The whole complex was covered with plastic bubbles interconnected by flexible tunnels; it looked like a veritable maze.

A man beamed at them as they approached the entrance.

"Roll up, gents, you're just in time. Don't want the hobgoblins to get you. Ten apiece gets you entry and access to the finest and most varied selection of rare entertainments ever offered to the public. When you hear what lies beyond this portal you'll—"

"Relax," said Kennedy. "There's only the two of us and we're coming in."

"Habit," said the man, taking the money. "It gets

you. And I can't get used to this crazy world." He looked past them at the deserted city. "Well, may as well close down and get some shut-eye."

Kennedy asked, "What happens if we want out?"

"You wake me up." The man gestured to a cot in an alcove beside the portal. "I've got to lock up—rule of the city—but who the hell would want to go out at dark-time?"

Certainly not the natives. The few Kennedy saw, a scatter of low-class servants, were crouched in nooks against the plastic, unable to afford the more expensive mobiles and unable to go home. Others, more wealthy, had taken refuge in the emporiums. Some of the natives Kennedy saw were probably their servants and bearers.

The Ultima Thule stood to the east, a tunnel running to it from a plastic hemisphere, a junction serving it and others. An officer weaved from it, a Cissurian clutching his arm, her voice a honeyed sweetness.

"A steam bath, friend, and a good meal. Some sobup pills and a couple of tapes to while away the time. More if you want it and can use it." Her tone was suggestive. "You ask, friend, and you get. Anything and everything that's going."

Anything for a price, that was, and he would pay dearly, Kennedy knew, but he would learn one day.

"Hey, man, you wanna try a fall with me?" A scarred amazon looked speculatively at Saratov from a bright and gaudy booth. "Ten gets you fifty if you can stay on your feet for three minutes. Double if you put me down. How about it, man? You willing?"

She thought it would be easy money for a little work; like so many others she had taken the giant at face value. He hesitated, tempted to teach her a lesson, then regretfully speeded up to join Kennedy at the entrance of the Ultima Thule.

"A hundred." The doorkeeper was firm. "That gets you in. Food and drink you pay for. You want a seat close to the stage that's extra. Arrange it inside."

The pulse of Kasedian rhythm stirred the air inside, a low throbbing coming from the stage, a small, slightly raised area. Facing it were seats arranged in a broken circle. Aisles radiated from the dais to a wider space containing the entrance, a long bar, a counter piled with food. Girls and men bustled up and down loaded with trays as they served the customers who filled the seats. Clever lighting accentuated the curves, giving the place a false impression of size; mirrors helped the illusion.

It was hard to realize that the whole thing could be knocked down, packed and loaded into the capacious hold of a ship. That, in fact, the structure against which it rested was a ship, slow perhaps and ungainly, yet capable of traversing the gulfs between the stars.

"Seats at the front?" The girl was pert, her eyes thick with glitter, the scanty costume she wore doing little to hide her figure. "You're lucky. I've a couple of cancellations. Two-fifty each."

"Robbery," rumbled Saratov.

"Supply and demand," corrected the girl. "If you don't want them, others will."

"At darktime?" Kennedy looked over the auditorium. The place, though crowded, was not completely full, and he saw more than two vacant seats in the front row.

"They'll be taken," said the girl, following the direction of his eyes. "When the main event starts you won't stand a chance. Zilma draws them like a magnet. Tell you what, I'll take four hundred for the pair."

Kennedy gave her the money, but held more in his hand.

"When is Zilma due on?"

"She's done one show. The next will be in a couple of hours. Time enough for you to settle down, have a few drinks and relax." The girl's eyes were on the money Kennedy held. "Anything more you want?"

"Yes. I want to see Zilma Narayan."

"You will, when she comes on."

"Privately."

"Forget it." The girl was emphatic. "No private visits."

"Not for five hundred?"

"Not for a thousand. If I tried to steer you to her I'd

get busted and dumped and, mister, this is one hell of a place to get stranded."

"You won't get stranded," said Kennedy. "I'm an old friend of the owner. How is Emil?"

He saw the shadow in her eyes, the indecision, then she said, "As always, but if you know Emil you'd better put the deal to him."

"I will. Where can I find him?" Kennedy peeled notes from the sheaf in his hand. "Let's get to it," he urged. "Here's a thousand. It's all yours if you'll just tell me how to get to the rear. If I'm questioned, you had nothing to do with it. That's a promise."

She hesitated for a moment, then, with an abrupt gesture, snatched the notes. "There's a door to the right of the stage. It's behind the curtain. Go through it. Turn left for the dressing rooms, right for the office. But be careful, mister, there are men in there who play rough."

"Fair enough," said Kennedy. "Now sit us close to where it is."

The seats were small and cramped. Saratov muttered as he wedged his bulk into the narrow accommodation. The music changed and became a subdued blur of background noise as an aging comic stepped on the stage to turn the air blue with his crude humor. A waitress came forward to take their order, fetched drinks, charged high and smiled at the tip.

"What comes next?" asked Kennedy.

"Boddari dancers and then a Zalech. Breaks in between for refueling. You want me, mister, you just wave."

"A clip joint," rumbled Saratov as he sipped at his glass. "Watered wine, crummy food and exorbitant prices. What's your plan, Cap?"

"I'm going to the rear." Kennedy glanced at the curtain and the hulking man who leaned casually against the wall before it. "When the dancers come on get up and go to the rear. Start a diversion."

"It'll be a pleasure, Cap. And if you don't come back I'm coming after you."

The lights dimmed and the music changed again. A

troupe of Boddari filed on the stage to writhe and twist in suggestive abandon. Saratov heaved his bulk from the seat and lumbered up the aisle. Kennedy heard a mutter of voices, a yell, the crash and splinter of breaking glass. A man cried out and a woman screamed. Heads turned as attention moved from the stage to the unseen drama behind.

The hulking man straightened and turned, scowling. He looked at the curtain, then back toward the noise. Coming to a decision, he left his post and headed for the disturbance.

Kennedy glided from his seat toward the curtain like a shadow, ducking behind the cloth and finding the promised door. It opened silently beneath his hand and he stepped into a narrow passage flanked on one side by metal, on the other by the flimsy structure of the stage. Turning left, he followed the curve of the passage. The sound of music diminished, dying as he reached and passed through another door. Dressing rooms ran in a line, the panel of one marked with a gilded star. Kennedy reached it, listened, then opened it with a smoothly coordinated action and stepped inside.

The girl was alone.

She sat before a dressing table framed with light, pots and jars of cosmetics before her, one hand holding a delicate brush with which she was painting her eyes. Neither her hand nor the brush faltered as she saw him in the mirror.

"Yes?"

"You are Princess Zilma Narayan?"

"I am." The brush lowered and she turned with a lithe movement on the backless chair. "Do you know me?"

Kennedy looked at the face, the eyes, the rippling waterfall of midnight hair, the sublime proportions of her body, the satin texture of her skin. He knew her, and he would never forget her. But her eyes had been empty windows before; now they were veiled, enigmatic.

He said quickly, "By reputation only, madam. I am Jak Tomlire, an entrepreneur specializing in the field of entertainment. I heard of your performances and, may I add, your reputation does you less than justice. Not only are you skilled, but your beauty is truly fantastic."

"As is your method of approach. Tomlire?"

"Jak Tomlire."

"A name which is strange to me. I could ask how you managed to penetrate to my dressing room, but no doubt you will tell me later. I assume that you have come on a matter of business. If so, you have wasted your time."

Her voice was soft, mellifluous, seeming to hold the delicate chiming of bells.

Kennedy said, "Perhaps, but I think not. To see you so close is reward enough. May I sit?"

He took a chair at her nod, eyes searching the room. It was small, with a screen to one side. Clothing hung on pegs, lay spread on a couch and showed from a partly open trunk. The disarray would be considered normal for such a room. The furnishings would not.

The rug was an expanse of Illranian web, the low table a product of the aquatic artists of Frule; the chair on which Kennedy sat would have cost more than any normal entertainer made in a year. A lantern cast a soft, yellow glow and the air was heavy with the scent of khan.

It was a nest of luxury to hold a pearl of price—an apt setting for a creature belonging to Kaifeng.

"You do well, Zilma," he said, gesturing at the room. "But you could do better. I can promise you a standard fee of—"

"Zilma?"

"Informality is normal in our profession, as you know, my dear. But if you prefer to be called Princess . . . ?"

"No. It does not matter. You were saying?"

"My offer. Let me put it this way. I will treble whatever you are getting now, and there will be a bonus—a percentage of the gate. One percent for the first three shows, then rising to five if the take warrants it. I think if safe to promise that it will. Within five years you could be rich. Within ten—"

"Ten?" She smiled and gently shook her head. "No, my friend. As I said, you are wasting your time. The bribes you gave to my supposed protectors have been to no purpose. You did give them bribes for such an invasion of my privacy?"

Kennedy parried the apparently casual question.

"There are ways. Now about my proposition . . ."

"No," she interrupted. "I am not interested in your offer."

"At least let me talk to your agent. You do have an agent?"

"No."

"To Emil Groach then. Does he still own the Ultima Thule?"

She said blandly, "I am remiss in my hospitality. Allow me to offer you some wine."

Her eyes met his as she handed him the goblet, a fragile thing of engraved crystal, the wine itself a golden orange. She stood for a moment, searching his face, then returned to her chair and said musingly, "Your face holds a disturbing familiarity. Have we ever met before?"

"Would you remember if we had?"

"Yes. I remember everything. But your face troubles me. I cannot place it and yet I am certain that I have seen it before."

"Perhaps on some other world," suggested Kennedy. "Perhaps when you were waiting for a booking. I may have passed by on business. Such things happen." He lifted the wine to his lips, not drinking, but pretending to swallow. "You have been on many worlds?"

"Several."

"And given performances?"

"As I do here. Now you must go. I have to get ready." She rose, tall, imperious. "It would be best if you left of your own volition. If not . . ." She broke off, shrugging. "There is a man outside who will escort you from the emporium."

A tall man with a blank, smooth face and a dull, uniform-like dress entered the room, a guard most likely summoned by an unseen signal from the girl.

He said, "This way, mister. Don't try anything. You'll regret it if you do." His hand dropped to his belt, the compact needler in its holster. "Just leave and don't come back. Understand?"

"I was only making her an offer."

"Which was turned down. Now move!"

There was no point in staying. Kennedy had learned what he had come to find, and the room had obviously been tapped or the guard could not have known of the conversation. And if someone had listened, others could have looked—Kaifeng perhaps, who would have recognized him at once.

Saratov was waiting at the portal. The doorkeeper woke, grumbling.

"You guys must be crazy, going out at a time like this. What's wrong with staying?"

"They go out!" snapped the man who had accompanied the giant, his needler aimed at Saratov's broad back. The guard who stood behind Kennedy ordered, "Open up and pass them through."

The door slammed behind them.

Darktime was all around.

It was strange and eerie, the pale light of the stars augmented by the shining halo of the eclipse. Thick patches of shadow filled the narrow streets of the town. The air was heavy, brooding with a nearly tangible menace, electric with unresolved potential. The silence was complete, a stillness broken only by the soft pad of their boots as they walked to where the jitney was parked.

"Cap!" Saratov drew in his breath with an audible hiss. "Over there!"

Kennedy followed the pointing hand. Nothing was to be seen.

"It's gone," said the giant. "But I saw something move."

"Illusion."

"Maybe." Saratov wasn't convinced. "I guess it had

to be, Cap, but it seemed real enough to me. And there! See?"

Kennedy spotted it that time, a hint of movement, the trace of jaws and a lumpish body, all half buried in the ground. The blur vanished as they watched.

Kennedy still wasn't sure whether it was a ghost of Epidoris or merely an illusion induced on their senses by the stimulation of unknown forces.

He said, "Let's get on our way, Penza. There's nothing we can do here for now."

The jitney was where they had left it. Kennedy unlocked the door and followed Saratov into the machine, activating the motor as he slammed the door. The engine whined, a thin, high-pitched note which undulated a little as they drove from the parking lot and down the road leading to the installation. The headlights cast a swath of brilliance ahead in the gloom.

"Cap!"

Something at the edge of the light reared, huge, massive, falling back as the road suddenly dipped, twisting with unfamiliar roughness. A boulder appeared before them, wavering like smoke in a wind. A tower rose in front of them, a delicate spire against the stars. It quivered, vanished, then reappeared in a blur.

Kennedy slowed as again the road unaccountably dipped. The note of the engine grew higher now, seeming to pervade every fiber of his being. The sound shrilled and then abruptly ceased.

"Cap!" Saratov shouted as the jitney bounced, dropping to land at a tilt. "What the hell's that?"

It was a creature from a nightmare. The thing had a body as large as a horse, crocodile jaws and a thick tail which swung like a whip to smash into the little vehicle, crushing in its side. The jitney rolled down a slope and landed with a grate of metal against the side of a boulder.

Chapter Seven

There were clicks and rustles and something which made a trilling sound. Kennedy stirred, feeling the throb and ache in his temple, the stiffness of dried blood on his cheek. Metal cramped his arms and chest; to one side the body of Saratov was a dully breathing mass. The jitney was on its side, the door bent, the window and the windscreen shattered, shards of plastic clinging to the frames.

It was daylight and the air was full of the scent of growing things. Through the shattered windshield Kennedy could see plants and trees and what seemed to be a trail.

It was indeed a mystery, but it would have to wait; the first thing was to release himself and Saratov from the wreck.

He twisted, freeing an arm, reaching to the lock. The door was jammed and he rammed his shoulder against it, pressing against Saratov as he heaved. Metal yielded and he gained more room. A second heave and the panel flew open.

The ground outside was soft beneath his feet and for a moment he leaned against the wreck, waiting for a sudden nausea to clear. He touched his temple and found matted hair, a shallow gash and some swelling, but the bone was intact. Straightening, he looked around.

A semitropical jungle stretched out on all sides, tall ferns interspersed with graceful trees, bushes bright with flowers and red fruit. The jitney rested against a boulder, the side crushed, Saratov's head lying in a pool of blood.

As Kennedy touched him he groaned, muttering, still unconscious.

The red fruit was a mass of pulp, sweet and sticky, crushing easily. Kennedy found a wide leaf, twisted it into a cone, filled it with juice and dashed it into the giant's face.

"Cap!" Saratov turned, revealing a torn cheek, a lacerated and bruised scalp. "My legs! I can't move!"

Metal had trapped him when the front of the jitney folded back like an accordian; a strut lay across his massive thighs.

"You're caught, Penza. Get your hands under that strut. Ready? Together, now!"

Metal lifted as they both strained. Grunting, the giant rammed his freed legs against the front of the vehicle and heaved. The seat bent backward as the frame gave under the push of his shoulders. Shaking his head, blinking, Saratov joined Kennedy at the side of the crushed machine.

"What happened, Cap? That thing . . ."

"It slammed against us with its tail. We hit a dip at the same time and landed against the boulder. We both got knocked out. How's your head?"

"It hurts, but I'll live." Saratov ran his tongue over his bottom lip. "What I could use is a drink of water."

They found a stream a hundred yards to the north, each washing while the other kept watch. Saratov's wounds, like Kennedy's, were shallow, cuts over the iron bone of his skull. The impact would have killed an ordinary man.

Back at the wreck he said, "What happened, Cap? Where are we?"

"On Epidoris."

"But that's crazy. The place is like a desert. Where did all this vegetation come from?"

"I don't know yet, Penza, but I'm beginning to understand." Kennedy looked at the sky. The dark sun had passed across its twin; the eclipse was over. "Did you

notice anything strange about the engine's sound when
we left the parking lot?"

"It varied," said Saratov after a moment's thought.
"It shouldn't have. The maintenance engineers must be
getting careless."

"Or something was done to it while we were in the
Ultima Thule." Kennedy gripped the machine and
heaved. "Let's find out."

Together they turned the machine right-side up and
removed the engine cover. Inside was the compact motor, wires running to the power source. Attached to
them was a small enclosed device.

It opened beneath Saratov's hands and he scowled at
what it contained.

"A sonic-emitter, Cap, set for a high frequency and
alternate variables spreading from, say, ten thousand cycles to maybe fifty thousand. Well above audibility in
any case. But what the hell was the point of fixing it to
our jitney? It couldn't hurt us."

"It moved us, Penza. It sent us over the edge."

"Into what?"

"Another plane of existence," said Kennedy grimly.
"It can't be the only answer and it's what must have
happened to the barracks which vanished. Those men
and that building couldn't have been moved in any normal fashion; they weren't wiped out by any known
force. They must have been transported from one plane
to another. And we can guess who was responsible."

"Kaifeng!"

"The girl was the same one I saw in his base, Penza.
There has to be a connection. I don't know if he identified us or whether he just wanted to try out that device.
Maybe it was simply a precaution on the part of his men
or it could even have been an accident. They must have
installed the thing while we were in the emporium. The
jitney came from the installation and anyone could have
been using it. Another disappearance of personnel could
have shut down the operation."

"Using the superstitions of the natives as a weapon,"
rumbled Saratov. "They wouldn't be scared of ordinary

death, but when the ghosts start to move in they'd go into a huddle. Ghosts," he said blankly. "Is that what they are, Cap? Creatures from another vibratory plane of existence impinging on our own?"

"Perhaps, but Epidoris is unique, Penza." Kennedy looked at the sky. The dark sun was continuing its passage away from its twin. "It's my guess that when dark-time takes place the entire planet is bathed in a radionic field which somehow weakens the bonds separating one plane of existence from another. A push, an additional impulse then, and matter can be transformed; it can even be sent from one world into another, almost identical world occupying exactly the same place in space and time, but not in the same phase."

He examined the soft ground and the trees, remembering the desert and scrub. They still existed, their atoms interspersed with those of the things he could now see and feel, occupying the empty space which made up the bulk of any matter.

Saratov lowered his arm. He had been trying to use the communicator without success.

"No contact, Cap."

"You can't send radio messages to ghosts, Penza. And that's what we are as far as the others are concerned now. Ghosts. But we're not alone."

Saratov looked expressively at the vegetation, the wrecked jitney.

"You're forgetting the others, Penza. The fifty-two men in the barracks. We'd better find them."

The trail Kennedy had spotted led in approximately the right direction as far as he could judge. He led the way along it, wary, remembering the beast which had appeared in the shadows. Leaves were torn and twigs lay crushed along the path, fruit pulped on the soft ground. The marks of clawed feet were plain. Insects hummed, their noises stilling as the two men passed, resuming after they had gone. A flying thing lifted on gauzy wings and something chittered in one of the trees, leaves falling to mark its hasty passage.

After fifteen minutes Kennedy paused, frowning. The

terrain was different from what he had expected, the trail winding now to the north. Without familiar landmarks it was impossible to be sure they were heading in the right direction.

A tree soared to one side and he climbed it, balancing on the swaying tip, eyes narrowed as he looked around. The vegetation was thick, a cloud of bird-shapes lifting from one side. He turned to face the direction in which he expected the barracks to be. He saw a low rise and the glint of something metallic.

"Cap!" Saratov's call was urgent. "Something's coming this way."

It arrived as Kennedy's boots hit the ground. The creature was long and vicious with feet clawing the dirt and wide jaws open to reveal rows of shining fangs. The scaled back stood as high as a man; the tail was a hammering club of flesh and bone.

Saratov ducked and sprang to one side as it charged, the jaws snapping air where he had stood. The beast halted immediately, its head turning, saliva dripping; the eyes, set far back from the snout, gleamed like emeralds.

"Penza!"

Its speed was fantastic, the long, lithe body as flexible as a cat's. Head and tail swinging, it snapped at the giant again as vegetation crashed all around.

Saratov jumped clear just in time, his foot turning as he landed, throwing him off balance. He rolled in a clump of bushes, thorns ripping at his robes as he struggled to his feet. Kennedy's hand slipped under his blouse, reappeared holding the flat weight of a sprom pistol. He lifted it and fired, the self-propelled missile lancing from the barrel, a thin thread of flame reaching to hit just at the rear of the monster's front leg, penetrating and exploding in a gout of flame.

Wounded, the creature reared, its head lifting, jaws gaping, turning to sweep its tail toward Kennedy's position. He sprang high as the tail cut through the air, but not high enough. A hammer slammed against his boot and he fell, head down, rolling, feeling the claw of thorns on his back and scalp. Caught in the bushes,

Kennedy twisted, lifting the pistol. At the same time Saratov rushed at the creature, a thick branch in his hands, the end oozing sap where he had ripped it from a tree.

It was a primitive weapon, almost useless even when driven by Saratov's powerful muscles, yet he hoped to provide a momentary distraction.

The sound of the wood as it crashed against the side of the crocodile-like head was that of an ax hitting stone.

Again the thing reared. Kennedy fired as the yellow belly came into view.

Spots flowered on the scaled hide, craters blown from the flesh, blood lacing a red trail from the impact of the missiles. They were small, their energy limited, but Kennedy sent others after the first, aiming at where he guessed the heart would be. Blood from torn arteries sprayed like a fountain, the detonations muffled now, the small missiles burying themselves deep before venting their charge.

"Penza!"

The thing was dying, internal organs ruptured, the heart ruined, but it was still dangerous. As Saratov turned, running, it crashed down and threshed with dying reflex, dirt pluming, bushes ripped from the soil and thrown high, the tail like a whip as it lashed the air, the very ground.

And, dying, it screamed, a high-pitched, siren-like cry which rose and lingered to hang suspended on the air. Abrupt silence followed as the creature gave a final jerk and lay still.

"Hell, I wouldn't like to meet one of those things in the dark!" Saratov stared at the huge carcass. "And that noise! Calling others, do you think, Cap?"

"That or a warning." Kennedy looked at the open jaws, the shape of the teeth. "It must be a predator, which means there can't be too many of them in any one area. That bulk would need a lot of food to keep going."

"And it was probably hungry." Saratov rubbed at his scratches. "If it hadn't been for your gun . . ."

. . . They would have been dead, hunted down no matter how fast they ran, crushed by the tail and torn apart by the jaws.

Kennedy examined the pistol, checking the load. The magazine was empty except for a single charge, and one shot would be useless against another such beast.

"We'd better get moving," he said. "That noise would have been heard for miles. It might attract the wrong sort of attention."

"Natives, Cap?"

"It's possible. There's certainly life here and there could be people." Kennedy checked their direction against the sun. "The barracks is somewhere over there."

They reached the building in just under an hour, moving cautiously, ears strained for the rustle of leaves, the impact of feet. It rested on a slight promontory, a shimmer of light reflecting from the metal of the walls. The entire building was slightly tilted on the uneven ground.

The door was open and it was deserted.

Saratov roved through the upper level as Kennedy searched the lower. As they met in the open area before the door the giant said, "Nothing, Cap. From the look of it the men just picked up their gear and went."

"Weapons?"

"Gone."

The men might have taken them, or perhaps they were collected later or even stolen; there was no way to be sure. Kennedy checked the drawers of the desk, seeing nothing but official documents, rosters, lists of names. A duty book lay to one side and he opened it, frowning at what he saw.

"The last entry is a package delivered by a native for Lieutenant Vickers. He had room twenty-six. Let's see if we can find it."

The compartment was undisturbed; only the ruin of the player marred the general neatness. Saratov frowned at it, dropping to his knees to make a closer examination.

"Fused and ruined, Cap. The whole instrument's

burned out and turned into slag. That could never have happened in normal operation."

"And abnormal?"

"No. The current-requirement is too small. You could blow a fuse or, if you overrode it, damage the heads and the reproducers, but that's about all. To get this result you'd have to load it with another energy source—a bomb designed as a recording."

"A part of a bomb, anyway," said Kennedy. He frowned, thinking. "Someone sent him a package. It could have held a recording. When he played it something happened—the same kind of thing that happened to us. But the barracks would have required a far higher impulse to move than a jitney with two men."

"Critical mass, Cap?"

"It could be. It's normal to leave favorite recordings stacked in the selector, and we know the lieutenant collected Zilma Narayan's. Four in all . . . but what if someone sent him a fifth? It was darktime, he would have been bored; it would have been natural for him to play it. And then, when it hit the others—"

"Bang," finished Saratov. "Or no, not an explosion, but maybe a pulse of some kind. An induced vibratory sequence which reinforced another one already created." He looked around the room. "Maybe we could find others, Cap, and check it out. Some of the men have players and they might have the recordings."

"But not the final one, Penza. That was a special delivery and one probably made just for the purpose."

The trap had surely been baited with the lure of Zilma Narayan.

Kennedy remembered how she had looked, soft and utterly feminine, smooth and graceful, the very timbre of her voice a subtle magic. It was hard to imagine such a girl willingly sending men to their deaths—if they were dead.

The answer rested outside, beneath a small mound of naked dirt: three men, their eyes glazed, blood on their uniforms, the broken shaft of a spear buried in the breast of one, savage cuts on the others.

"Murdered," said Saratov. "But how, Cap? They would have been armed and wary. How did they get killed?"

"By surprise," said Kennedy softly. "Don't move, Penza. They're all around us."

Chapter Eight

They stood like shadows in the vegetation, tall, thin men with peaked hair and down-slanted eyes, mouths pursed beneath flaring nostrils of snubbed noses. They carried narrow spears tipped with dull metal; long, heavy knives with waved and tapering blades hung from their belts. They wore dull garments blotched with green and brown, camouflage which rendered them invisible to a casual eye.

And, on the breast of each, rested the symbol of a double helix limned in yellow.

"Kaifeng's men!" Saratov's voice was a deep rumble which rolled in the strained silence. "Cap—"

"You will not move!" The voice was thin, harsh, determined, the words oddly accentuated. "You spoke of the master. Do you know him?"

"Yes," said Kennedy. "Were you sent to escort us?"

The question aroused confusion. There was a blur of sound, odd noises in a peculiar guttural tongue, and then the harsh voice again.

"You will lift your hands. If you move you will die."

They stepped forward as Kennedy and Saratov obeyed. Penza, thick arms lifted, said, "The natives, Cap. They must have heard the beast and come to investigate."

"Or maybe they have been looking for us." Kennedy glanced to either side as the natives approached. He caught a glimpse of others in the shadows; their squat, powerful-looking crossbows were lifted, dull metal quarrels aimed toward the two men. The one who had spoken halted ten feet from where they stood.

"If you come from the master you will have a sign. Show it to me."

"We have no sign."

"Then you have lied." A hand lifted and spears were raised. "You will be taken to him. If you resist you will join those others in the dirt." His eyes slid to the opened grave. "Now we shall tie you."

"Cap, do we stand for it?" Saratov was ready to fight.

Kennedy glanced at the poised crossbows, guessing at other weapons the vegetation might conceal.

"We stand for it, Penza. They're taking us where we want to go anyway."

Bound, prodded by the butts of spears, they were marched through masses of vegetation, following an almost invisible path. Twice the column halted as something moved in the distance; the natives conferred among themselves in guttural whispering, then moved on with renewed urgency as the danger passed.

They reached a valley, a patch which seemed more swamp than solid ground, a slight rise and then an open space.

"Cap!" Saratov stared at the building it contained. "How the hell did these people ever manage to build that?"

The structure was vast. It was composed of thick columns positioned in an elaborate pattern, tapering as they rose, interweaving, complex. The roof was like a shallow bowl, a flattened dome on which elaborate patterns of metal rose to an encircling fringe. The area surrounding the building was bare, the edge of the vegetation sharply defined. Figures were busily working, plucking fragments of green from the naked soil. As they drew closer, Kennedy saw that the workers were women and girls, their skirts lifted and caught at the waist, tattoos marring their naked torsos.

The circular wall of the building was pierced with doorways, the jambs rising to pointed arches. Kennedy slowed as he looked at the space between two of them, recognizing the familiar pattern engraved deeply in the stone—the convoluted, interwound circles which comprised the Zheltyana Seal.

A spear butt slammed against his spine and a hand thrust him forward into a doorway. The chamber beyond was a huge vault in which the blur of whispers echoed like the drone of bees.

"Reporting," said Saratov. "They're handing us over." He tested his bonds. "I could break these, Cap."

"Not yet, Penza." New captors were walking toward them, tall, haughty men armed with Diones. The insignia they wore was a scarlet flame against the dull green of their tunics. "I guess they're going to take us to Kaifeng."

He was as Kennedy remembered, tall, dressed in rich maroon with golden braid in a writhing pattern, the gemmed insignia of a double helix on his breast. Seated on a throne-like chair, he radiated an almost tangible air of icy menace, an impression heightened by the coldly chiseled perfection of his features.

Drawn taut over prominent bone, the delicate skin seemed to be made of rare porcelain. The remote eyes were large and radiant, the emerald irises flecked with crimson, the orbs elongated and slanted upward beneath finely arched brows. The nose was thin, the mouth a gash over a rounded chin, the ears small and set neatly against the domed skull.

Wei Kaifeng, the most dangerous man Kennedy had ever met, leaned a little forward in his chair, staring. The sound of his inhalation was loud in the small chamber in which he sat.

"Kennedy! Captain, this is indeed a most unexpected pleasure."

"Unexpected, Doctor?"

"I assure you that it is so. Had I known you were on Epidoris I would have devoted time to arrange something of interest." The cold note held a feral purr, satisfaction changing into an acid promise. "I have been badly served. Those who have failed in their duty will pay."

Kennedy knew he meant they would pay with torment, screaming agony and unbearable pain. Bodies would be distorted perhaps, left alive to crawl mewling in a cage, a spectacle to intrigue the curious, a warning to those who guessed the truth.

Kaifeng's reputation was soaked in blood.

He said softly, "I owe you much, Captain. If you had five lives you could never repay the debt. And fate is with me, is it not? Here you are, bound and helpless, delivered into my hands. An irony, Captain, as you must agree. And yet we must be practical. A man should not be blamed for the attributes which make him what he is. Tsing!"

A man glided from the shadows behind the throne, broad, squat, his face a mask of stone.

"Master?"

"Remove the gross one. Hold him fast."

Saratov's muscles bunched, one of the cords snapping with a thin, high sound. "Cap!"

"Go with him, Penza." Kennedy knew that escape now was out of the question. The throne was fitted with instruments of destruction; the touch of a button would flood the area on which they stood with nerve-twisting radiation.

"A wise decision, Captain," said Kaifeng as the giant was led away. "You, I have reason to know, can withstand pain to a remarkable degree. But the other? Perhaps we shall determine that question at some later date. It would be an amusing incident with which to beguile the time. Possibly you will be able to witness it."

A gong murmured as he touched a button set into the arm of his chair. To the man who answered the summons Kaifeng said, "Remove those bonds and serve wine to my guest."

It was a ruby-shot yellow, strands of scarlet lacing the amber fluid, drifting as if holding a life of their own.

Kennedy looked at it, then shook his head.

"You are cautious," said Kaifeng as the servant glanced questioningly toward him. "A laudable attribute, but I assure you the wine is harmless. And even if it were poisoned, what have you to lose? A few more hours of continued existence? A few more days? Years, even, what does it matter? Death will come one way or another. What is it that makes life so important to a man that he will cling to it no matter how unbearable it has become? An interesting question, Captain, and another one which I one day hope to answer."

"A man lives because without life there is nothing," said Kennedy. "The basic need to survive has little to do with abstract philosophies."

"And always there is hope," mused Kaifeng. "The elusive promise that, one day, all will be well. That is the weakness which makes rule possible—that and the threat of pain which turns the most arrogant into abject slaves. These things can be used."

They had been used, but by none more viciously than the man on the throne. Kennedy looked at him, knowing his weakness—his overwhelming pride which made it necessary for him to talk, to boast, to display his talents. The warped genius needed an audience.

"The wine," said Kaifeng. "Drink it!"

"Master." The man bowed and, lifting the glass to his lips, drained the contents.

The act proved nothing to Kennedy; the antidote could already have been administered.

"Coincidence," said Kaifeng, musingly. "Of all the worlds in the galaxy, you had to come to Epidoris. It seems that your luck, Captain, is not as it was."

"Perhaps not," said Kennedy. He rubbed his wrists where the bonds had cut deeply into his flesh. The sprom pistol with its single load had been taken from him; if it hadn't, Kaifeng would now be dead. "But you? What brought you here? The legends?"

"You want me to talk because there are things you hope to learn. I do not underestimate you, Captain, and yet it will do no harm to satisfy your curiosity. What brought me here? A new world!" Kaifeng's gesture embraced the room, the building, the planet outside. "One in which I am free to do exactly as I please. This world will be the fountain of my empire. You know, of course, of its unique attribute? The delicate balance of forces which exist during darktime, when the vibratory bonds are weakened and transition is possible?"

"A natural curiosity."

"No!" Kaifeng's voice rang through the chamber. "Not natural, Captain. Not wholly so, at least. This building in which we sit—can you guess how old it is? Old beyond our imagining. You saw some of the natives —do you imagine they could have built it? The very concept is ludicrous. They are animals, content to breed, eat and sleep. They have fire and can barely work metals. But they will learn. I am already teaching them."

"And they accept you as their master?"

"I *am* their master!" Kaifeng rose, imperious, regal. "Always, everywhere, I am the master!"

His egomania was verging into egotheism, Kennedy noted. Kaifeng was convincing himself that he was supreme, that the galaxy existed for him to rule, that he was a god. His overwhelming ambition, coupled with his genius, had already made him the danger he was.

"I shall rule," said Kaifeng, more calmly. "Here and elsewhere. Those who oppose me will cease to exist. Those who serve me will do well."

Kennedy said, "The building?"

"A machine, a nexus of force which accentuates the natural field and alone makes full transition possible. You see, Captain, I am open with you. This place was built long ago, I think, in order to save this world and its people from the effects of the bright primary going nova into a white dwarf. It is still operating in a way. I determined its existence and discovered how to use it."

Kaifeng stepped from his throne and gestured to Tsing, who had entered by some hidden panel, to stand beside him.

"Come," he said to Kennedy. "Let me show you the thing which will give me the rule of all."

It was as if they were ants walking through a radio, the rooms themselves taking the place of transistors, condensers, conduits, circuits. The walls were sloped in mathematically precise planes, the roofs distorted in subtle configurations, the shape of each compartment following unknown equations.

Slabs of different materials covered every surface, the floors mosaicked in red and amber, black and silver, blue and gold. Even the jambs of the doors were twisted to follow a pattern unimaginably old.

"As far as I can determine it is a solar receptor," said Kaifeng, toward the end of the tour. "At the time of nova, when the twin suns were in eclipse, it must have discharged its accumulated energy. This would have created the spatial warp which literally moved the planet into a coexistent plane. It moved the surface, at least, but that was enough. The vibratory scale was altered for a time so the flood of destructive radiation could be rendered harmless."

"So an alternate world was created, in a sense." Kennedy frowned. "But the power required would have been tremendous."

"And available," reminded Kaifeng. "What could be more powerful than an exploding star? And true creation was not necessary; all that was required was to alter the vibratory rate and send all life into a different phase. The planet in the normal universe is a sere and barren ball of rock and sand barely able to support life. This is a comparative paradise."

Of course, Kennedy reflected, this was a paradise in which Kaifeng was the serpent. He would use this world to hide men and ships, to build fleets and equip them, emerging on a wave of conquest which would leave peaceful worlds in flame. He could operate from here, but he could never be harmed.

Chapter Nine

Captain Shaffeck was regretfully firm. "Veem, I'm sorry, but there is no more we can do. I've had men scour the road into town a dozen times. Fliers have checked for a hundred miles to either side. We've used metal scanners, the lot. The jitney has just vanished and they went with it."

"Anything from the workers?"

"Rumors. We've tried to keep it quiet, but you know how word gets around. A jitney's missing, the natives in maintenance noticed it. It isn't in town, therefore the ghosts got it. We're lucky it wasn't anything else."

"Lucky!"

"Lucky," repeated Shaffeck firmly. "If another building had vanished, or even some of the regular personnel, we couldn't have held them. You may not like it, Veem, but there it is."

Fuming, Chemile left the office. The operation was working at full blast outside, open vehicles carrying natives between the base and town. They had refused to work unless transport was provided—another worry for Major Rebner.

Halting at the site of the vanished building, Chemille checked the equipment and instruments Luden had set up: plates, receptors, radiometers, sensors, magnetic detectors, apparatus of a dozen kinds. The professor was in the *Mordain* busy compiling a mass of data.

"Anything, Veem?"

"No. Shaffeck hasn't found a thing. In fact he said it was lucky that only Cap and Penza were involved."

"A perfectly natural reaction from his point of view." Luden's fingers danced over the keyboard of the computer as he fed data to the machine. Touching a button, he pulled the print-out from its slot. "As I suspected, Veem. During darktime there is a strong electro-gravitational field with evidence of a temporal shift in phase."

"Which means?"

"Matter as we know it is strongly held by both space and time conjunctions in the continuum; to move one you must alter the other. It is as yet impossible to send a fragment of matter from one point to another instantaneously. There is always a time-lapse. That is why the temporal shift is most important. It bears out the possibility of an alternate phase. We exist now," Luden explained, his voice adopting the dry tones of a man lecturing a class of students. "But that period which we term 'now' is a moving vector. We are always in the future; we move even as the very concept of 'now' is formed. If not we should remain in a status where even the very process of thought would be impossible. Now imagine that, somehow, a man or an object could be made to lag behind a little. What would be the effect? Not a return to the past, because the past will have progressed forward and the past, by definition, must be in stasis. It is a theory, I will admit, but one based on logical assumption. Therefore, if an object or person could be thrown back a fraction of a second it would no longer be to our present 'now.' It would have, as far as we are concerned, vanished."

"Is that what happened, Jarl?"

"I can't be sure, Veem. I personally tend to doubt if that is the answer. A movement was certainly made, but in which direction is still open to question. Surely not in the ones we know and, I hesitate to believe, in time. Which leaves"—he paused, his eyes clouded with thought—"the Relcarg phase theory. But in that case there would have to be a nexus."

Again he busied himself with the computer, looking up only to nod as Chemile brought him coffee. Irritable, restless, Chemile hit the button on the monitor and listened again to the recorded sounds from the speaker: the noise of the fight transmitted by Saratov's communicator, the conversation Kennedy had held with the girl, the peculiar sounds of the jitney.

As a final thin, undulating wail came from the machine Luden looked up from his papers.

"Veem, play that again!" He listened intently, checking the time-span of the sound.

In the abrupt silence Chemile said, "That's when it happened, Jarl. Right smack in darktime."

They had been busy with the instruments then, the monitor set to automatic register. It was a normal situation; the speakers could have been activated by a touch of a button on one of the disguised communicators.

Luden now said, "Veem, take a recorder and get the normal working tone of a jitney. Take it at varying speeds and over different terrains. While you're doing that I'll isolate the tone of Cap's vehicle."

"You've found something, Jarl?"

"I'm not sure and we haven't enough data as yet. Please hurry, Veem."

The instruments on the *Mordain* were of the highest quality; the tone Luden obtained was clear of all electronic noise, static and fuzz. He listened to the jitney sounds Chemile had obtained, then set up apparatus, twin feeds, a screen, oscilloscopes, amplifiers, delicate verniers.

Working, he explained.

"That undulation could have a bearing on the disappearance of the jitney, Veem. It sounded foreign to normal working and I want to get a precise pattern of the exact cyclic variation."

"It could have been just a fault in the motor, Jarl."

"Perhaps, but we must check it out regardless. I'm using a visual monitor because I feel that what we heard was only part of the actual vibration."

"Sound."

"Sound is vibration, Veem," snapped Luden impatiently. "A pattern impressed on the air or other medium which we can recognize. But the human ear can only receive a narrow band and I want to get it all."

He threw switches and adjusted the verniers. Two patterns showed on the screen, thin trails which peaked and dipped.

"The lower is the recording you have just made, Veem, the upper is the one from Cap's vehicle. See how they differ? Above the regular pattern is another. Now if we can correlate the two motor-sounds and eliminate them, we should be able to isolate the extraneous vibrations." Luden's fingers were deft as he worked. The screen blurred, then cleared to show a single pattern. It was irregular, broken with high peaks and valleys, the band a fuzz of varying intensity.

"There it is, Veem. A most complex pattern, but one we should be able to reproduce."

"And then we can go after Cap and Penza?"

"No." Luden was definite. "It might be possible for us to build a device capable of matching that pattern, but there are variables which must be considered before we could hope to reproduce the identical situation. Even if we did, we have no evidence that we would go anywhere; or if we did move, that it would be to where they are now. In any case, Veem, how would we be able to return? No, all we have acquired is another fragment of data to add to the rest."

"But, Jarl, they could be in trouble! Needing us!"

"I am fully aware of that possibility," said Luden grimly. "But action without purpose is wasted energy. It will not help Cap if we enter without the means to either give aid or return. Now I want to make a check on each of the available recordings of Zilma Narayan. It is obvious that she is a creature of Kaifeng's, and we know Lieutenant Vickers was interested in her. Set up the player, Veem, full-band reproduction. We can do without the visual."

The four recordings were each played again and again, the sound checked over the entire range above and below the spectrum of audibility, familiar notes eliminated, the patterns filtered, correlated one with the other . . . hours of work for a negative result.

"The recording medium itself, Jarl," suggested Chemile. He picked up one of the disks and flexed it in his hands. "Could there be something in the material itself?"

Luden had a machine grind one to powder, then assembled apparatus to analyze the dust, delicate electronic probes to quest for traces of latent energy.

He frowned at the results.

"A peculiar stress-pattern, Veem, of unusually high potential. It could possibly be triggered by the application of a complex vibratory sequence. But we have no idea as yet of what the key could be."

"Maybe he received another recording, Jarl, the trigger."

"It is possible," said Luden slowly. "In fact I would say most probable, but it doesn't help us. We have no way of knowing where it came from or what it was."

"We don't know, Jarl," agreed Chemile, "but we can guess. Zilma Narayan would have the answer. I'm going to find out."

It was nearing day's end and the vehicle which took Chemile to town was filled with men eager to sample the pleasures of the assembled emporiums. Chemile paid the doorkeeper and moved toward the Ultima Thule. A placard announced the cancellation of the dancer's performance, and men turned away grumbling; others shrugged as they paid their fee.

Chemile joined them and edged his way toward the stage—then apparently vanished as he pressed himself against the curtain. Behind him he heard the mutter of voices, the click of a door, and a hulking man stepped from the hidden panel. As he took up his position, Chemile slipped past him through the door, freezing as a guard glanced toward it.

Frowning, the man tested the catch, opened the door a little, then slammed it shut. His actions gave Chemile all the time he needed to pass on down the passage, taking the right-hand fork at a guess.

He froze at the sound of voices.

"But, my lady, the take! Unless you perform, the gate will be nothing!"

"You dare to argue!"

Emil Groach felt himself cringe beneath the cold lash of the girl's voice. Sweating, his face creased in an ingratiating smile, he said, "Argue, my lady? No. I merely point out that—"

"Enough!" She stood before him, tall, chill, her feminine softness masked by the clothing she wore: the tunic high-collared and long-sleeved, the breast gemmed with the symbol of a double helix. The mass of her hair was piled in an elaborate crest. She said bleakly, "You will obey. In all things, at all times, you will obey. If you have forgotten, then perhaps another lesson would be in order."

"No!"

"The prospect terrifies you?"

"My lady, please!" He was almost babbling, his face gray with fear. "I wish only to serve."

"The guards who should have protected my privacy the last darktime will be returned to you shortly," she said casually. "I doubt if you will recognize them and, of course, they will be unable to speak. Study them well, Emil Groach. As they are, so you could become."

"I—" He broke off, swallowing, then said weakly, "I have done my best to please. Ever since you bought the Ultima Thule and . . . and . . ."

"Showed you the path you must take?" Her smile was devoid of humor.

"Yes. I learned, my lady, there is no need for you to threaten."

"Nor, I hope, to remind. Leave me now. Go!"

Chemile slipped into the office as the door opened. He pressed himself against the wall, blending into the background, thankful that the girl had turned away from the portal to sit at the desk. She touched three points on its surface, and a hidden drawer slid from one side. She took out a thin sheaf of papers and a wide belt fitted with pouches and instruments. Glancing at the papers and then her watch, she set dials and strapped the belt around her narrow waist.

She slammed shut the drawer and crossed to the door, opening and closing it before Chemile could move.

He hesitated for a moment, then cautiously opened the panel. The girl was far down the passage; no one else was in sight. Softly he followed her, reaching another door, a flight of stairs, then a passage which had been dug from the ground. The walls glistened with fused sand, highlighted by the cold bluish glow of Kells.

It led to another, much older, passage. The floor was worn and the walls and roof were blotched by black patches, the legacy of a time when it had been lit by naked flames, torches set into holes gouged in the sides.

This passage turned, circling, branching, straightening after a while to slope upward—part of the maze which ran beneath the city. A door creaked as Chemile began to climb and he froze as the girl turned, his back against a wall, even his breathing stilled.

Light shone past him and around him. Satisfied she had not been followed, the girl snapped off the beam and passed through the door into the darkness outside. The air was still, holding an eerie mystery.

And the girl vanished.

She disappeared as if she were a cloud of smoke, one second standing limned against the stars, the next wavering, thinning, seeming to move at an incredible velocity, and yet not moving at all. Then nothing.

Chemile stood looking out for a long moment before turning back toward the door. It was thick with ancient timbers and straps of iron, set into the side of a low mound which broke the desert on the far side of the town. Chemile guessed that it was an escape route, or an emergency entrance for those who had strayed too far and were unable to return before the curfew.

He closed it after him and retraced his steps, finding the newly dug passage and climbing the stairs at the far end. A single guard patrolled the corridor and Chemile waited until he had turned before gliding through the door and following him. He froze when the man turned, waiting his chance to enter the office.

Deftly he touched the points on the surface of the desk, remembering their positions, the sequence the girl had used. The drawer slid open and he lifted the papers, pushing back the compartment until it locked with a soft impact of metal. The sound covered the opening of the door.

"You—" Emil Groach stood in the opening, his eyes wide, startled. "What the hell are you doing in here?"

Chemile was moving before the question was asked, his free hand lifting, the fingers clamped, the bone and muscle of palm and wrist turned into a pointed club. As Groach opened his mouth to shout the fingers stabbed into his larynx. Gasping, fighting for breath, he lifted his hands, but slumped as Chemile chopped at the side of his neck. Sensitive nerves numbed by the impact, he lost consciousness and thudded to the floor.

"Emil?" The voice of the guard echoed from the passage outside. "What happened? Is something wrong? Are you—"

He broke off as he stepped into the office, lips thinning, one hand jerking the needler from his belt, eyes narrowing as he searched the apparently empty chamber. Chemile waited against the wall, the papers held behind him. He would be trapped if the man had the sense to shut and lock the door; instead the guard stooped over the prostrate figure on the floor.

"Emil! What happened, man?"

Chemile quietly glided from the room.

Chapter Ten

The pit was twenty feet deep and twenty feet across at the base, too wide to straddle and too high to jump. The stone walls narrowed at the top to an opening five feet across. They were fashioned of smoothly fitted mortared blocks which gave no hold, tapering inward as they rose. The floor was solid rock, covered with dirt and fetid slime.

To one side lay a huddle of bones, skulls grinning with silent mockery; natives who had been thrown into the pit and left to starve.

"Nice company," said Saratov. "They were all over the floor when I arrived. I cleaned up a little." Like Kennedy, he had been stripped and given a scanty loincloth. "Kaifeng's idea of humor. I'd teach him how to laugh if I could get my hands on him."

Kennedy made no comment, remembering the journey from the building to the pits. He had been marched over the cleared ground toward the huts of a native village which showed at the edge of the vegetation. He's seen grilled openings with guards standing on watch—tall natives armed with spears and heavy knives, and others, not natives, carrying holstered Diones. They had watched as he had been thrown into one of the pits, their faces blank, impassive.

Creatures suborned by Kaifeng's manipulations, their brains had been adjusted to rob them of feeling, to leave them with no other emotion than the wish to obey.

"When they brought you here, Penza, did you get a chance to look into the other pits?"

"The one next to this, Cap. I pretended to stumble and managed to get a look inside. The light was bad, but it holds men. I think they must be from the barracks." Looking at the wall, he added, "I can't see how we can get to them. Even if I threw you up to the grille it wouldn't do any good. The guards would stop you from calling."

"We've got to contact them," said Kennedy. "Look around, there could be something hard lying loose."

He found it beneath the heap of bones, a stone as large as his fist. He tapped the wall, listened, tapped and listened again. After a long while he heard a response, taps in the universal space-code.

"Who?"

"Kennedy. You?"

"Lieutenant Ormond. Out?"

"Maybe. Can dig?"

"Try."

A shadow blocked the opening as a guard peered down. A woman next to him lowered a thick earthenware pot at the end of a string. It snapped as Saratov caught it, the end rising to leave the pot in his hands. It held water.

"How about some food?" he yelled as the grille slammed back into place. "I'm hungry!"

There was no answer; the grille was vacant, thick bars across the sky.

Kennedy said, "The water, Penza."

He tasted it cautiously, finding it warm and a little brackish. It could be drugged, but that was a risk they had to take. Thirst was already making itself felt: soon they would be parched. He drank before handing the remainder, more than half, to Saratov. It was a fair division, since the giant's frame needed more fuel than a normal man's.

As his companion lowered the empty pot Kennedy said, "Break it. Large pieces if possible."

Saratov grunted, clamped his hands on the edges and jerked. The pot shattered, leaving seven sharp-edged fragments of baked clay. Kennedy selected one and went to the place where he had tapped. The point of the shard made a harsh grating sound as it scraped between the blocks. The mortar was old and thick, powdering quickly. Within minutes they had dug a deep channel around one of the blocks.

Crossing to the heap of bones, Kennedy selected a long, jagged shard as his next tool. It was relatively fresh, adding to the depth they had reached.

"Right, Penza. Now it's up to you."

Saratov crouched, his fingers rammed into the cracks they had dug. Muscles bunched on his shoulders, standing in ridges on his back, swelling his biceps and forearms. His feet rasped against the powdered mortar on the floor, thighs like the boles of trees as he pulled. The block shifted a little, grating, then moved a little more.

Saratov pushed it back, freed it from the other side, moving it backward and forward, loosening it in its bed.

And then, gripping, he pulled.

Blood darkened his nails, oozed from the tips of his fingers. Cords and ropes of muscles stood clear beneath his skin as, with a sudden jerk, he pulled the block from its setting. He fell backward with a grunt, throwing the mass of stone to one side.

Rising, he peered into the hole, seeing another block, a twin of the first.

"Cap, warn them to stay clear and then support me."

He threw up his legs as Kennedy took his weight, pressing the soles against the block as his hands dug into the opening to find a grip. Sucking in his breath, he straightened, pulling and thrusting at the same time. Already weakened from the other side, the block fell clear to show a face, a pair of bloodshot eyes.

Lieutenant Ormond was in a bad way.

He crawled through the opening and straightened, wincing a little. A wad of crushed leaves was held to his right side with sticky gums; his back was laced with the ugly pattern left by a loaded whip.

Kennedy nodded as Ormond explained what had happened.

"And after? When you discovered that you were in a different place?"

"I sent out a seven-man patrol, armed and with orders to be careful. Just to make a limited scout and report after a couple of circumnavigations. We found three of them at dawn and buried them. The others?" He shrugged. "No trace."

Killed and left for the predators to find, Kennedy guessed, or perhaps allowed to escape. The end would have been the same.

"And?"

"There isn't much more to tell. We'd finished the burial and then they were all around us. Kaifeng's men, but I didn't know that at the time. We could have put up a fight, but there seemed to be no point. We needed help and they promised to give it. Then, on the way, we were jumped and disarmed." Ormond added, grimly, "If I'd known what was going to happen we'd have fought to the last man. It would have been cleaner."

Kennedy could guess how he felt, seeing proud men tortured, tormented, enslaved, whipped. He said, "What have you learned?"

"Not very much. Kaifeng wants Epidoris left alone; he doesn't want the flood of trade and people that will arrive once the installation is completed. Myaz Sharn can be swayed, and if he won't move he'll be pushed, assassinated, even, but I guess you know all that."

"Anything else? The building? Kaifeng?"

"The man's crazy, if you can call him a man." Ormond was bitter. "I think he's a sadistic devil. He asked us to work for him, to train the natives in basic military disciplines, stuff like that. A few of the men gave him the razz. He took them, flayed them and hung them up on trees. They were still alive and screaming when he did it. Then he gave us the treatment." His hand jerked up to point at the whip scars. "Then he asked again, one man at a time. The first one refused. He was impaled. I didn't give the second a chance to be a hero. I don't mind fighting if there's a chance, but we had no chance. It was agree or be killed. So I agreed."

"You did right."

"I hope so. Now he's got half of us working while he keeps the rest of us in the pit as hostages. Anyone steps out of line and we all get it." Ormond looked at his hands; they were trembling. "I don't know how long we can last, Cap, but something's got to happen soon. If it doesn't there won't be any of us left."

"How many men do you have?"

"Thirty-two."

"How about local conditions?"

"The natives go for him, at least some of them. He coasted in on a legend, you know, the powerful being of the past returning to aid his favorite children. But I think some of them are getting disillusioned. They don't like what he does and they don't like to be forced to work. The old chief is out in the jungle and he's got men with him. He might be persuaded to take a hand, but what good are spears against Diones?"

Kennedy said thoughtfully, "That building is pretty old. There must be a religion based on it. Are there priests?"

Saratov rumbled, "Cap, how would he know?"

"I know," said Ormond. "One of the men I work with, a native, told me about them. From what I can make out they welcomed Kaifeng when he first arrived. He taught them the language and they thought it was the god-tongue. He used hypnotechs and they lined up to learn. That's where most of his local guards come from, the priest-class. To them he's a real god: he gives them things and promises more. It's the old chief who has been put out. He was once the kingpin, now he's nothing."

Kennedy knew he could put such a potentially explosive situation to good use. But the natives would have to be stiffened with men who could set an example. As warriors they would still be of limited use against sophisticated weapons, yet their numbers would count. A gun could only hit one target at a time.

"When they bring back the others from their work," he asked, "what happens?"

"They put them into one of the other pits. Then we all get fed. Tomorrow we'll take their place. It's turn and turn about."

"And guards?"

"Only a few at night. They don't like the dark. Kaifeng's men go into the building."

"We'll break out tonight," said Kennedy. He glanced at the grilled opening; the bars were already growing indistinguishable against the darkening sky. "Get back to your own pit and pass the word. Listen to the signals and obey them. Once out and free, head for the jungle and find that chief. Get him to attack. Guerrilla warfare, you know what needs to be done."

"And Lieutenant Vickers and his men in the other pit?"

"We'll get them out if we can." Kennedy met Ormond's eyes. "But only if we can. This is no time to be gentle. Kaifeng has to be stopped."

"And after? Even if we somehow manage to win, Cap, how are we going to get back where we belong?"

"We'll get back," said Kennedy. "Just don't worry about it for now."

As Ormond wriggled back through the opening, Saratov dubiously asked, "Do you think we ever will, Cap? Get back, I mean."

"Kaifeng must have an installation of some kind in the building so he can move from one plane to another. We'll take it and use it."

Night came with the throb of drums from the native village. The ruby gleam of dancing flames from fires lit well away from the pits threw flickering shadows over the grille. The food was scant, a small portion of something like cheese, a nutty paste and a few orange fruits. They ate and waited for the external noises to die. Only when he judged that the guards would be careless did Kennedy act.

"Penza!"

Saratov locked his hands, stooped a little and, as Kennedy rested his foot on the open palms, lifted with a smooth explosion of energy. Kennedy rose into the air, hands catching at the wooden bars. They were as thick as his forearm, slippery and hard to hold. Hanging, it was impossible for him to raise the grille, but the opening into which the bars were set was five feet thick, room enough for him to wedge his body.

Feet to one side, neck and shoulder to the other, he pressed upward, feeling the grille lift, moving it to one side as it cleared its bed.

Cautiously, he looked over the edge.

He could see a standing shape against the glow of the distant fires, another to one side, a third barely spotted in the starlight. He looked toward the building, now bathed in a pale shimmer of radiance, a thin, greenish light which clung to the columns and the roof. Tall figures showed clearly at the base of the structure.

Kennedy tensed, calculating. The men would be looking toward the fires; the glow of the building was like trapped moonlight, bright to him, but illuminating only the ground immediately at the foot of the building. The guards by the fires, dazzled, would see little, but if he rose he would be clearly silhouetted against the light.

Kennedy relayed what he had seen to Saratov, adding, "I'm going to try it, Penza. Pass the word for the others to be ready."

A quick move and he was hugging the ground, ears tense for the sound of an alarm. None came and he crawled away from the building toward the shapes he had seen: first the one in the shadows, then the one nearest, finally the one before the fires. Time would pass before he was missed; firelight was deceptive.

The first man tensed as a leaf rustled. He turned to receive the slash of a stiffened hand across the side of his neck. Kennedy caught his spear as it fell, drew the heavy knife at his belt and passed on. The knife was bloody by the time he reached the third man, bloodier still when he moved on.

The next part was harder. Rising, he walked boldly forward, lifting the spear as the nearest guards turned.

"Hold!"

"Who comes? Who . . ." The words dissolved into a stream of gutturals.

Kennedy said, "A message. Gather close. The master orders it."

"Kaifeng is great!"

"All life to Kaifeng!"

The first went down beneath the flat of the blade, the second took the point in his heart. The other, not as close, turned and ran.

The thrown spear caught him, sent him falling, his open mouth filling with dirt.

"Cap?" Ormond's face was at the grille as he stood on a human pyramid. "Out?"

"Out." Kennedy lifted the grille. "There are dead guards by the building; get their weapons. The rest of you move toward the village where there are more. Send someone back with the guards' clothing. Hurry!"

Trained, disciplined, they acted with swift efficiency. Men rose from both pits, some thrown by Saratov, who was the last to remain. Clothing knotted into a crude rope was lowered and he climbed out.

"Cap!" Ormond rose from the ground. "What about the others?"

"Get away from here!" snapped Kennedy. "Take your men with you. Damn it, you know what to do. Do it! I'll take care of the rest."

Vickers was in the last of the row of pits. He eased himself painfully over the edge, gasping, rolling to one side. His men followed, swarming up the rope, obeying Kennedy's whispered instructions. "Up!" he snapped at the officer as the last man slipped into the darkness. "Move!"

"I can't! My back—"

It was torn, scarred, oozing blood and pus from a lattice of wounds. Kennedy wondered how he had ever managed to climb the rope—his men, he realized, had lifted him.

"Try, man! Try!"

Saratov grunted as a shout came from one side. The sound echoed, repeated. From the building came a sudden beam of light, brilliant and hard. It traversed the ground close to where they stood, missing the giant's sprawled shape by inches, halting as it illuminated a running man.

The blast of a Dione tore the air, releasing a shaft of searing energy from unstable atoms. The charge, contained by magnetic fields, directed and focused by permanent magnets ringing the barrel, reached out to touch the running figure. It lanced through the skin of the back, the fat, and the spine, burning a path through living flesh.

"Cap!"

Other guns opened fire as Saratov called, filling the air with the thunder of their discharge, illuminating it with released energy. Men died as they ran, falling, smoking, the scent of charred flesh rising from their bodies.

"Cap! That fool—"

Vickers had risen to his feet and was running, a staggering figure, his back a parody of lace, a picture framed in the light which moved to embrace him, the guns which cut him down.

"Penza!" Kennedy's voice was sharp. In seconds the light would find them, the Diones finding an easy target. There was only one place they could go. "Into the pit! Move!"

Chapter Eleven

Lying supine on the operating table, bathed in a cone of light, the native looked like a broken doll. Liquids had bathed his skin, ultraviolet light sterilizing the pores and cracks in which bacteria could lurk. His shaved head showed the indentation caused by the flat of Kennedy's blade.

Zilma Narayan laved it with a sparkling blue fluid, picked up a scalpel and, with deft strokes of the keen blade, cut a flap away from the scalp to reveal the naked bone. It was shattered, broken edges pressing on the brain, sharp splinters thick with ruptured tissue. She used a trephine to cut a wide circle around the area, lifting the freed segments with forceps and dropping them into a dish containing a nutrient fluid.

The native stirred, muttering a little, and she checked the pulse and respiration. A hypogun lay on a tray of instruments and she picked it up, firing a charge of numbing drugs into the base of the neck; the blast of air carried the compound through skin and fat into the bloodstream.

From where he stood in the shadows Kaifeng said, "That was unnecessary. The clamps are sufficient to hold him."

"True, but the noise was a distraction."

"Fear," mused Kaifeng. "He can feel nothing—the spinal anesthetic robbed all feeling—but the fear of the unknown still persists. How extensive is the damage?"

Swinging a magnifier into position, she stared intently at the exposed brain. The bone had cut deep, leaving lacerations and burst cells, masses of pulped and oozing tissue. The gray-white cortex was mottled with clots of blood.

"Not minor. It is a wonder he is still alive. Only the thickness of his skull saved him." Lifting her head, she stared at the tall figure at the edge of the illuminated area. "I would like to do what I can. I need the practice."

"Continue."

He watched as she returned to work, noting the skill with which she used a variety of instruments to cut away the damaged tissue, staunch the flow of blood, sear cells with a medical laser, neatly repair the torn membrane. She smoothed the removed bone on an abrasive disk, filling the gaps with a paste. The compound hardened as she worked and would harden even more with the passage of time, creating a thin, external coat which would blend into the living structure. The bone fitted and sealed, she replaced the flap of skin and flesh, suturing it with a laser. Aside from the thin, three-sided rectangle of the wound, there was no evidence of the delicate surgery.

"You are deft," approved Kaifeng. "But why did you take such care to remove the damaged cells? Searing the area would have sufficed."

"True, but the scar tissue would have produced a barrier-node to the reestablishment of the injured neuron paths."

"And would have been a latent source of future trouble," agreed Kaifeng. "But such care was unnecessary. Now that the man has been treated, what will you do with him?"

"Return him to his family as a gift." The girl examined the naked scalp, then, satisfied, sprayed a transparent dressing over the thin red lines. "He will experience difficulty with muscular coordination," she murmured. "He will be partially paralyzed and have double vision, but the effects will not last for long."

"No." Kaifeng was coldly amused. "They will not."

"Doctor?"

"The man was a guard. He failed in his task. That cannot be overlooked."

Zilma Narayan stripped off her surgical gloves, threw them to one side and looked at the supine native. Her wide lambent eyes were devoid of emotion; the man had presented an interesting medical problem, that was the sole limit of her interest.

Casually she said, "That is true, Doctor, but to be merciful—"

"Is to be weak!" His voice rang through the chamber, little echoes whispering, accentuating the sudden harshness of his thin, cold voice. "The strong must never be weak—it is a luxury they cannot afford. What is promised must be done and the penalty of failure can never be lessened. Return this man fit and well and he will be an example to others to be careless in their obedience. A problem, Zilma. Resolve it."

Quietly she said, "Here Kaifeng is the lord of all. He gives and he takes. Life granted as a reward can be taken as a punishment."

"Elaborate."

"The man has been healed and his family will be grateful. Their spirits will be raised from the depths to the heights. Yet his failure cannot be forgiven; he must be punished. Delayed, it will have a greater impact."

Kaifeng smiled, thin lips curving in cruel anticipation —an expression utterly devoid of humor.

"He will die," he whispered, "slowly, turned into a thing of nightmare, begging for release from pain. His suffering will be a public spectacle to warn all that I must be obeyed. It pleases me to hear you say it, Zilma. Those who stand close to me must be strong."

"You doubt that I am strong?"

"No." He stared at her with cold appraisal. "You are a creature of my making, formed and fashioned for a purpose. I have given you skills and knowledge which set you apart. You are a chalice containing a part of my being—an extension of myself as is my hand, my arm. And yet, should you defy me, I would not hesitate to strike you down."

She met his eyes, tall and proud, radiating her arrogance, her ruthlessness.

"There is no need to threaten me, Dr. Wei. I obey."

"Yes, Zilma, now and for always you will obey." Kaifeng glanced at the native. "Let us leave this carrion. For two days his family can rejoice and then he will pay."

Tall, resplendent in his robes, Kaifeng led the way from the chamber. Tsing stepped from the shadows to take his place at his side and a little to the rear, an attendant guardian. The girl fell back a little as they headed for a ramp, a winding strip of humming metal on which danced tiny flickers of emerald fire.

Above was a room containing maps, instruments, massed apparatus, everything touched with the greenish luminescence. Centered in the chamber was a low dais ringed with parabolic reflectors, their bowls filled with a milky shimmer.

Blank-faced men stood at various instruments, guards and technicians wearing dull tunics emblazoned with the double helix.

One turned, bowing as Kaifeng approached.

"The potential is falling, master, but the anticipated residual level will be higher than before."

"The rate of drain?" Kaifeng nodded at the answer. To the girl he said, "All is as I expected. The energy loss matches the force used to effect your transfer. The attractive effect of the nexus has been successfully demonstrated."

"The alignment was not exact."

"That is immaterial. Once the potential has been raised to a sufficient level it will be possible to counteract the negating effects of the daytime field and enable transposition to take place at all times."

"If the correlating instruments are correctly tuned," she reminded. "Have you solved the mass-ratio problem?"

"Almost. It is, unfortunately, geometric: twice the mass requires four times the initial stimulus. However, once the potential is raised and maintained, adaptions can be made. I see no insurmountable problem. All is proceeding as planned."

A table supported a large-scale map, details in red superimposed on others in green. Kaifeng studied it for a moment, then tapped various places with the tip of one finger.

"At the next darktime transitions will be made at these localities. Men must be stationed in readiness. See to it."

"Master." A man bowed.

Another man at a different piece of apparatus said, "Master, we have lost trace of the men who escaped. Extrapolating from their last known position, it would appear they are heading toward the camp of Scheel Ulet."

"Action?"

"I have ordered out patrols and trebled the guard, master."

"Send a party to the chief and bring him to me. Take gifts. He may come attended, but I will brook no refusal." To the girl Kaifeng casually said, "Those men who escaped, how would you set about recapturing them?"

He must already have the answer to his problem, she guessed; his question was a means to test her.

Impatiently she said, "It is simple. A heap of goods will be offered to the natives for each man returned. That is the carrot. The whip?" she shrugged. "At each hour starting at dawn a man will die until they are all returned, either alive or dead. How many escaped?"

"Twenty-seven, madam," said the man at the instrument. "Five were killed."

"Five?" She frowned. "But that leaves—"

"Two others were found in a pit," said Kaifeng. "A most ingenious method to avoid death and discovery. It would have worked had I not suspected what could have happened. A search revealed them. I want you to meet one of them in particular."

Kennedy stood in the chamber with the throne, tall, hard, his near-naked body stained with dirt and blood.

Guards stood close, needlers aimed, their eyes watchful. To one side a giant was bound with thick cords. He was as soiled and as stained, the purple of bruises blotching his shaved skull.

She gave him one glance, then stared at the taller figure.

"Jak Tomlire."

"A name," said Kaifeng. "But he uses many names. Allow me to introduce you to Captain Kennedy. A man who is not wholly what he seems."

Kennedy watched as she approached, seeing the lithe grace of her, the dancer's skill reflected in every movement. And yet this was no ordinary entertainer. About her hung something of the alien chill of Kaifeng. She halted, her eyes searching his face; she was so close that, stepping forward, he could have touched her. Her eyes were a little puzzled, a little curious.

"Strange," she murmured, "how I seem to remember you, and yet I cannot place when and where we met." She glanced to where Saratov stood, apparently passive, yet in reality a coiled spring ready to explode into action should the opportunity arise. "You I do not know." Dismissing him, she looked again at Kennedy.

He said dryly, "We shall know each other again if ever we meet."

"You think that possible?"

"In the universe all things are possible, or didn't your master teach you that?"

"My master?"

"Kaifeng." His eyes held her own. "Or do you labor under the delusion that you are his equal? If you do, forget it. To him all other living things are inferior."

"Which is as it should be," she said flatly. "Until another can prove himself the stronger, Kaifeng will rule."

"The right of might."

"Natural law," she corrected. "The concept that all men are equal is demonstrably false. Some are destined to rule and others to obey." She turned to Kaifeng. "Why are you showing me this man?"

"Because I have found him to be unique." Kaifeng

turned, went to his throne and sat with his hands resting on the arms. "How do you take a man, break him, bend him to your will? With pain, the great teacher which governs all. No matter how dedicated a man might be, how determined to resist, pain, intelligently applied, will shatter his resolve. This I have proved times beyond number. Only once have I failed. Guards!"

They backed, tense and wary; the girl stepped to the side of the chamber to stand at their rear. Facing the throne, Kennedy tensed, knowing what was to come.

"I failed," whispered Kaifeng. "But perhaps I will not fail again."

A button sank beneath his finger.

Kennedy fell.

He dropped to his knees, feeling the lash of the invisible electronic whips searing his nerves and his muscles, tearing at his sinews, the very fiber of his being. A drill ground at every tooth, nails scraped his naked bone, vices clamped on each finger, tightening, tightening . . .

"Any other man would now be screaming his throat raw," mused Kaifeng. He leaned forward, his eyes narrowed as if studying an interesting specimen, his face suffused with a peculiar satiation, as if he fed on the pain he had induced. "He would be begging for respite, pleading with me to end his agony, eager to talk, willing to obey. And yet, you see, the captain does not scream."

"An unusual high pain level," said the girl coldly. "Increase the intensity."

Kennedy doubled, his head lowered, every nerve a writhing torment. Only hard discipline learned over the years enabled him to maintain a precarious control. The Ghengach System of Disorientation divorced his mind from his body so that he floated in a strange detachment; the Clume Discipline gave him mastery over heartbeat and respiration, partially enabling him to block the impulses which carried the agony-stimulus to his brain.

"He could be broken," said Kaifeng softly. "I am almost tempted to try, to search out the very limits of his capability. Yet that would mean searing his nerves and leaving him irreparably ruined. Yet observe, Zilma, how even now he resists." His voice hardened, became a command. "Kennedy, you will acknowledge me as your master. Say it! Say that I am your master!"

Aside from the ragged breathing, the soft drop of falling perspiration, there was only silence.

"Higher," snapped the girl. "Increase the intensity. Break him!"

Kennedy straightened a little, lifting his face, anger not agony dominant in his eyes. Slowly he moved crawling toward the throne, climbing to his feet with exaggerated care, his muscles twitching, jerking as he fought to master his body. He took one step toward the seated man . . . a second, a third, his hand lifting, stiffening, the edge poised to chop at the neck beneath the ivory-mask of Kaifeng. Here was a man intent on killing, a man blind to everything aside from his determination to reach and destroy the source of his agony.

For a moment everything froze; only Kennedy moved, slowly, like a robot, the guards watching, not believing what they saw.

And then their weapons lifted, needlers loaded with poison-tipped darts. Two men had Diones.

"Cap!" Saratov's voice was a roar. "No, Cap! No!"

Cords snapping around him as he strained, one arm tore free. A guard fell with his face masked in blood; another doubled with broken ribs lacerating his lungs. Then something popped and a pale vapor wreathed the giant's head from a leveled projector. Like a stricken bull he crashed to the floor.

Kennedy ignored the shout, the noise of action, unaware of everything but the need to complete the task he had set himself, blind and deaf to everything but the man before him.

For a moment Kaifeng watched, savoring the sight, then he lifted his finger from the button.

Kennedy dropped, jerking in reaction from the tremendous strain, over-tried nerves and muscles jangling, knotting in bunches. Cramps left him helpless, not seeing the expression on the girl's face as she stared at him.

Cap! She had heard that name before, a name which fit the vaguely remembered face. That trigger had activated her memory.

"No!" She stepped forward as again Kaifeng reached for the button. "You have proved your point. Greater intensity would only kill."

"And that would bother you?"

"It would be a waste. I agree with you, Doctor, this is a most unusual man. It would be a pity not to investigate his potential further."

"You are interested?" Kaifeng looked at her, then at the figure slumped before him. He brooded for a moment, then, coming to a decision, nodded. "I agree that to destroy him would be a waste, but waste or not he must die unless he is willing to serve me. I do not think that you can succeed—the strength which makes him so valuable will work against you—but it will do no harm for you to try."

Rising, Kaifeng stepped down from the throne.

"Attend to it, Zilma. And if you fail, think of a suitable manner for him to die."

Chapter Twelve

The air was cool and scented with khan, the voice a soft susurration. It had been going on for a long, long time, repetitive words containing a masked suggestion, the concept that it would be best to relax, to cooperate, to obey.

Kennedy listened to it, knowing that it was a recording, an attempt at hypnosis. He guessed that he had most probably been given associated drugs, but if so their effects had worn off. He had no doubt as to their failure: his conditioning would make any attempt at hypnotism a waste of time.

He rested, eyes closed, feeling the firm texture of the couch on which he lay. His skin felt clean and he could feel the touch of garments, a blouse, pants and shoes of some soft material. Aside from aching muscles he felt well.

He could only guess how long it had been since he had collapsed in front of the throne of Kaifeng.

He opened his eyes cautiously and saw a low ceiling, walls painted a dull green. Rising, he found himself in a small, windowless chamber. The recorder whispered from under the pillow of the couch, ceasing as he listened.

"So you are awake." Zilma Narayan stood in the open door. She wore a simple gown of luminous violet, the color matching her eyes. A narrow band of jet held the dress firm to her waist. The fingers of both hands were adorned with heavy rings. "How do you feel?"

"I ache."

"You were fortunate not to have suffered from bro-

ken bones and strained cartilages. Muscular contraction
when induced by electronic stimulis can be most severe.
The safety factor is overridden and the result can be
most unpleasant."

"You talk like a doctor."

"I am a doctor." Stepping back, she gestured for him
to enter the other room. "Please, a warning. If you
should attempt to be violent the consequences will be
most unpleasant. For you, naturally."

"Of course."

He halted as he passed through the door, looking at
the luxury of the far chamber. Paintings rested against
the walls, delicate examples of Usifi art. A mass of per-
petual blooms slowly opened and closed their petals in
multihued brilliance, their scent wafting like fragrant in-
cense from the bowl of laminated hylet shell in which
they stood. Waves of diffuse color rose from a luxorgan,
a kaleidoscope of varying intensity shot with streaks and
shards of shimmering luminescence, sparkles and flashes
of coruscating scintillation.

He watched for a moment, then turned to the girl,
smiling.

"Schnitzler's Celestial Symphony. The third movement?"

"The fourth. The fifth and eighth chords are repeated."

"As a counterpoint to the third and eleventh," he
agreed. "A fascinating work in which Schnitzler attempts to portray mankind's rise from the sea to the
stars. I say 'attempts' because, as yet, no work has ever
managed to do more than touch the surface of the subject. Are you conversant with the poetry of Umbillia
Obonga?"

"Yes." She crossed to a low table, poured wine and
handed him a glass. "You remember what happened?"

"In the throne room? Yes."

"You will be pleased to learn that the experience has
left no ill effects. Incidentally, I must congratulate you on
your physique. You have a superb development." Rais-

ing her glass, she added, "Shall we drink to your continued good health?"

The wine was cool, tart and refreshing, holding a subtle acridity which, he guessed, was the product of some exotic herb. He deliberately took the glass from her hand and refilled both, handing her back the one he had used. If she noticed the switch she made no comment.

She said, "Let us talk. I am interested to know why you hesitate to join Kaifeng. Is it a personal matter or do you have other, conflicting loyalties?"

Hypnotized into a desire to obey, Kennedy would not have hesitated to reply. Immediately he said, "A little of both, I guess. What do you know about him?"

"Kaifeng? He is a genius."

"True, though I would have said a warped one. He uses his undoubted talents to achieve personal gain."

"As a rich man he uses his money to achieve personal power." She waved aside the objection. "Do you believe that the end justifies the means?"

"Sometimes. It depends on what end you have in mind."

"At the moment it is to persuade you to join Kaifeng, to convince you of the wisdom of doing so."

"The offer was made to me once before. I refused then. I am not inclined to accept now."

She said urgently, "Cap, you are a fool. What is the purpose of throwing away your life when you could have so much? A man like you is destined to be great. Work with Kaifeng. Stand at his side. Together we could rule the galaxy."

"To what purpose?"

The question surprised her. "Surely to rule is reason enough."

"For some perhaps, but not for me." Kennedy met the shining eyes, recognizing what he saw. Gently he added, "Why are you so concerned? What do I mean to you?"

"Nothing," she said quickly, then repeated it as if to convince herself. "Nothing."

It was a lie, but she herself had no way of telling its extent. Her memory, awakened, had placed his face, his name, in their correct context—the first things she could remember, the very first items of information impressed on her newborn mind.

A baby would have forgotten, but she had not been a baby. She had been full-grown, ready to step from the artificial womb of her casket . . . and a newly born animal will always consider itself akin to the first living object it sees.

And Kennedy fully intended to exploit that weakness in any way he could. His life, the lives of others, depended on it.

"I cannot understand," she said wonderingly. "You are an intelligent man. Continue to defy Kaifeng and he will destroy you. If necessary I will do it with my own hand. Your brain could be removed and kept alive and aware in a crystal jar. Your internal organs could be displayed on external trays. Death can come in many forms, even a living death: to be maimed and crippled and left to crawl blind and speechless. All this could happen—and will unless you agree to give your loyalty to Kaifeng, to acknowledge him as your master."

"And you want me to do that?"

"Yes. Yes, I do!" She frowned. "And yet I don't know why I am so concerned. You are a man, nothing else, yet somehow you seem more than that to me. But make no mistake, what I have said will happen. Answer me now. Do you agree or not?"

He hesitated for a long moment, watching, judging. The fraction of advantage he held was a frail thing; even putting it into words could dissolve the bond. And she would do as she had threatened, maybe allowing the knife to slip at a critical moment, saving him from horror, yet killing him just the same.

Shrugging, he said, "It seems you leave me no choice, Zilma."

"You agree?" Pleasure made her radiant. "I knew you would. And now you must show that you mean what you say. A simple test, but you must not fail it."

"And that is?"

"To kill your companion."

Saratov hung in a cage suspended ten feet above the ground from poles thrust deep into the dirt. It stood close to the jungle at the edge of the cleared area. Made of stout wooden bars lashed with vines, it was too small for him to stand or lie at full length, forcing him to squat with his knees drawn up to his chin, a position which would result in painful cramps.

Kennedy said, "How long?"

"Has he been in there?" The girl was casual. "Two days. This will be the third night. But why does it matter?"

Kennedy looked around, not answering. It was late in the day, dusk already blurring details and casting a somber gloom over the area. The only light was that thrown by the brightening glow of the building, which revealed strange fruit hanging on the trees, the cause of the stench that filled the air.

The men were dead and decaying, some burned, others with lolling heads and protruding tongues, a few patterned with dried blood from savage cuts. A row of corpses dangled from the trees, natives who had died so others would recapture the escaped prisoners.

Some had been taken. Kennedy saw two staring heads mounted on sharpened stakes, the body of a third impaled nearby.

He asked, "Is that all?"

"Yes. Scheel Ulet has not cooperated. The patrol sent to get him never returned." A chill frost edged the girl's mellifluous voice. "He will suffer for his disobedience when he is found. And now, Cap, do what has to be done."

"Is there any hurry?" Kennedy turned to look at the building. Casually he said, "I take it that the transfer mechanism is inside?"

"Yes."

"And Kaifeng's ship?"

"You ask too many questions. All will be explained

later." She moved, a little impatient. "This air is nauseating. Hurry, Cap. Once it is done we shall have plenty of time to talk."

He moved slowly toward the cage, eyes narrowed as he calculated the odds. Beside him the girl stayed just beyond reach of his touch; behind him the three guards in attendance stayed well back. They all held Diones in their hands, muzzles lowered yet ready to swing up and level.

They would shoot him down if he tried to run, not killing him, but burning the legs from beneath him, leaving him crippled and helpless for Kaifeng's revenge. If he tried to reach the girl, to seize her and hold her hostage, they would shoot just the same. She, like himself, would suffer the penalty of failure.

He remembered her warning, the calm acceptance of her fate.

And yet she had been confident and he could guess why. For two days or more he had lain drugged and exposed to hypnotic conditioning. She could not know of the barriers which had long ago been implanted in his mind against just such an eventuality.

There was a chance, another to add to the first, her inbuilt feeling toward him. Together they might just make her a little slow, a little reluctant to see him destroyed.

Above him, in the cage, Saratov moved a little, groaning. He had gone two days, almost three, without food or water, cramped in a limited space, exposed to the heat of the sun, the chill of night. This was the friend he was expected to kill.

Kennedy said loudly, "A problem, Zilma. How do you expect me to kill him? With my bare hands?"

"Could you?"

"I doubt it. He is very strong. Have you a weapon?"

"Drey!"

One of the guards moved forward at her command, his companions automatically following. He took an extra Dione from his belt and handed it to the girl.

"Here!" She threw it toward Kennedy. "Use this."

Catching it, Kennedy moved on past the cage toward the edge of the jungle, turning when he was a few feet from the vegetation. The girl had followed him, standing well clear now, too far for him to reach. The guards, watchful, stood almost beneath the cage.

Saratov moved a little in it, looking at Kennedy, then at the guards.

"A difficult shot," mused Kennedy. "The light is bad and the angle awkward. Perhaps if I moved a little to the left?"

The girl followed him, the guards changing position, turning, edging forward a little, now almost directly beneath the cage.

Two more steps and they would be right under it. If the Dione was loaded, if it would fire, Kennedy could burn through the supporting rope and send the cage crashing down on all three.

He said, "Perhaps if I moved closer? Could the cage be lowered?"

"No." She was frowning. "Why do you delay?"

"No reason."

Kennedy lifted the gun, aimed and closed his finger on the trigger.

Nothing happened. The gun, as he had expected, was empty.

He said coldly, "What is this, a joke?"

"A precaution." She came toward him, smiling. "But you didn't know the gun was empty, Cap. You aimed and fired, willing to kill. You can still kill. A word to the guards and they will do it. Just one word. Give it!"

"Penza! Now!"

Kennedy sprang forward as he shouted, hearing the rip of wood, the splinter, the snap of parting fibers as the giant strained against his prison. Zilma turned, looking toward the sound, recognizing her danger too late, falling as Kennedy's fist slammed against her jaw.

He turned as she fell, lifting and throwing the empty Dione in a blur at one of the guards, a man more cautious than his companions, who had jumped back and was lifting his Dione.

The missile caught him high on the bridge of the nose, slamming across his eyes, the heavy metal smashing bone and tissue, blinding, sending the shattered forehead back into the brain.

The cage shattered as Kennedy spun around and Saratov fell in a rain of heavy fragments which knocked down the other guards. Before Saratov was on his feet Kennedy was racing forward, stooping, snatching up the fallen weapons, firing as he straightened, twin shafts of searing destruction lancing from each hand.

Men died beneath the spears of raw energy, falling with holes seared into torsos and faces, intestines burned, bone charred, brains cooked, hearts ruined.

Then came a moment when the sudden onslaught was unopposed, a few seconds during which natives ran screaming and blank-faced guards dived for the ground, tearing at their holsters.

Above the thunder of the Diones Saratov's voice rose in a yell as he climbed to his feet.

"Cap!"

"Run!" Kennedy moved, blasting a crouching man, turning a face, a hand, a leveled Dione into smoking ruin. "Hit the jungle! Fast!"

He backed as the giant obeyed, hopping, staggering, fighting cramped muscles in the desperate need for speed.

A Dione blasted from high on the building, dirt pluming inches from Kennedy's feet, another shot singeing the hair as it passed close to his head. He returned the fire, spinning as Saratov yelled, long legs thrusting at the ground as he ran into the jungle.

Craters suddenly blasted the soil behind and to one side—threads of fire spouting from the sprom cannon. Gouts of flame exploded from the dirt and leaves fell from trees swaying as the missiles tore their boles with the fury of their impact.

"Cap! Here!"

Saratov was crouched behind a tree. He caught the weapon Kennedy threw toward him and fired as guards came running, providing a masking fire while Kennedy dived for cover.

A man fell, another, then the sprom cannon ceased to fire as the gunner recognized the danger of hitting his own men. That was a mistake, since he could have destroyed the area and all it contained at the cost of a few lives.

But the guards were bad enough.

They came crashing through the undergrowth, firing, mistaking shadows for men, men for shadows. Kennedy saw them rise, painted, camouflaged, firing with Diones, using spears and heavy knives. In seconds it was over.

"Cap!" Lieutenant Ormond was sweating, perspiration tracing paths over the dirt which masked his face. "We were watching, trying to figure a way to rescue Penza, but you saved us the trouble."

"Casualties?"

"Three men dead, sir," reported a sergeant who looked like a savage, his chevrons painted on his arms with juice. "Two hurt, neither badly. I've set the men collecting weapons."

"Make it fast," snapped Ormond. "Twenty seconds and we move."

On the way he explained where they were going.

"I've made a deal with the old chief, Cap. Scheel Ulet's given us shelter and guides in return for training his young men. He's interested in loot too, and he hates Kaifeng. We managed to get the patrol which was sent out to collect him and now he realizes he's in a bind. He either helps us, moves, or waits to take what's coming. If he moves he'll be a poor relation barely tolerated by the ruling chief. If he waits—well, he knows what's happening to the villagers. By helping us he's taking a gamble that we can defeat Kaifeng and put him back in top-dog position."

"How many men can he supply?"

"Not as many as I'd like. The young ones are eager but lack training. The hunters are good, but a little too careful. They like to hit and run. Good enough for attrition, but not so good if we hope to launch a major assault." Pausing, he added questioningly, "I guess that's what it'll have to be, Cap?"

"Yes," said Kennedy. "We'll have to take the building."

"It won't be easy."

"But it will have to be done." Kennedy was firm. "And soon. The way back is in there." He looked at the sky, the stars which were beginning to show. "We'll attack at darktime."

Chapter Thirteen

The flier was a general-purpose carrier, the pilot phlegmatic. For hours he had sent the craft back and forth over an area which included the town, sitting slumped in his seat, more a part of the machine itself than a living, thinking creature.

Now, it appeared, his passenger was satisfied.

"That's all," said Luden. "You can return to the *Mordain.*"

Chemile was waiting. He helped to unload the instruments from the flier, restraining his curiosity until both they and the professor were inside the ship.

"Jarl?"

"Success, Veem." Luden was tired, his thin face drawn, traces of red about the eyes. "I have managed to isolate the node of maximum potential. There had to be one, according to the Relcarg phase theory, a nexus of force containing the maximum weakness of the vibrational bonds. It is just here." His finger tapped a map covered with notations in his neat calligraphy.

"About where I saw the girl vanish?"

"Exactly, Veem. The instruments she carried must have been tuned to the nexus; their power, coupled to that of the transdimensional force, enabled her to pass from one phase into another without having to wait for darktime. The figures you obtained show this to be a fact. They contain not only the essential coordinates, but vibrational settings and harmonic cycles."

"Does that mean we can cross over, Jarl? Find Cap and Penza?"

"Theoretically yes, Veem. But, as I pointed out before, it will not be of much use for us to go empty-handed."

"Can't we make instruments for individual use?"

"Given time, perhaps," admitted Luden. "But I think I have a better way than sending a MALACA task force into that other region. If my calculations are right it will be possible to move the *Mordain* from one phase to another. However, in order to do that, we shall need Captain Shaffeck's assistance."

The officer frowned as he listened to what Luden had to say.

"All available recordings of Zilma Narayan? Sure, I'll sweep every room and locker for them, but do you think they will do any good?"

"Without them we can't hope to succeed," said Luden thinly. "Given time it might be possible to emulate what they contain but, Captain, we have very little time. I want everything to be ready at darktime. And don't forget that the fifth recording is the one most essential. If I guess correctly, some of the officers will either have them already or will have them delivered close to that period. I want them delivered to me as soon as they arrive."

"Will do, Jarl." Shaffeck made a note and then added soberly, "Is there any chance of getting Cap and the others back?"

"I think there is a very good chance."

"Do you need any help? Extra men? I can get a hundred volunteers if you give the word."

"No." Luden softened the refusal with an explanation. "It is a matter of mass. In order to do as I hope we shall need three complete sets of the recordings. To carry extra mass would necessitate another set at least. And then we have the problem of return. The time factor is critical and I have no way of knowing what the mass-stimulus ratio will be on the other side. We shall be taking a chance as it is; should we fail it is better that as few men are involved as possible."

The communicator hummed. Shaffeck answered it, then looked at Luden.

"Major Rebner wants to see you," he said. "Shall I tell him you're on your way?"

"Do that, and please get to work on finding those recordings. Have them taken to the *Mordain*. Veem will accept them."

Rebner looked more harassed than before. He waved Luden to a chair and began to pace his office as he spoke.

"I'll give it to you straight, Jarl. I've been in touch with Myaz Sharn. He intends to pull out all his workers if anything happens this darktime. If one man or machine vanishes, then it's the end of the operation."

"A bluff?"

"Maybe," admitted the major. "But I don't like to call it. Is there any way you can operate from inside cover? We could throw up a plastic envelope and—"

"It wouldn't work." Luden was definite. "I am sorry, Major, but that is out of the question. I must be at the very nexus and that lies to one side of the city. You realize why this is essential, of course?"

"I'll take your word for it."

"A mistake, Major, you should never do that," said Luden evenly. "All data should be checked and rechecked on a personal basis. However, I shall leave my figures with your technicians in case of need."

In case anything went wrong, he meant, and Rebner knew it. He slumped into his chair, looking at the professor with new respect. Some of the men, he knew, found the frail scientist an object of humor, but no man who was prepared to venture into the unknown was worthy of anything less than regard.

"There has to be an installation of some kind on the other side," said Luden. "It is, of course, invisible to us, but I have plotted traces of the energies it contains. These energies reach maximum at darktime when vision, at least, can pick up objects and things from the other vibrationary world. Hence the superstition of ghosts. It is even possible that, should a man be whistling, say, he might actually cross if he was at the right place at the right time and hummed or whistled the right series of notes. It would be a coincidence, but they happen."

"And?"

"And in order to eliminate the ghosts and to prevent Kaifeng from using that other world as a base, that installation must be destroyed."

It was simple put like that, but Rebner was not deluded. There would be men, weapons, defenses to protect the machine. And, above all, there would be the danger of never being able to return.

He said grimly, "If we could use the forces of MALACA Nine there would be no problem. We could vaporize the whole damned place."

"You could," agreed Luden. "But as you cannot there is no point in idle speculation. However, there is one precaution you can take. Have the condensing system constructed so that it will give a low, infrasound vibration."

"A blanket coverage," said Rebner, understanding. "Now, about Myaz Sharn?"

"Talk to him. Tell him that we are making a test. Promise him that, if we are successful, the ghosts will be eliminated forever." Luden rose. "I leave it to you, Major. Now I have other work to get on with and there is little time."

Too little. Darktime was close when Chemile had finished sorting the recordings and placing the three players at carefully selected points throughout the *Mordain*. Scowling, he looked at the sky, then at the road leading to the city.

"No sign of any messenger yet, Jarl. Suppose he doesn't come?"

"Logic tells us that he will, Veem." Luden had joined Chemile at the open port. "The political situation has reached a climax; if Kaifeng can cause more disappearances then the operation will be suspended, Myaz Sharn deposed and Epidoris will secede from the Terran

Sphere." He frowned at a patch of dust in the distance. "This could be the messenger now."

He was young, breathing deeply, a native who was proud of his speed and mission. Chemile moved forward as Shaffeck intercepted him.

"I'll take those, friend." The captain held out his hand. "Special delivery?"

"To be placed in the hands intended," said the native. "The names are plain. I was promised money."

"You'll get it." Shaffeck jerked his head toward one of the barracks. "And you'll be staying here during darktime. Don't worry, we'll make you comfortable."

"No!" The native recoiled, his eyes wild. "This place is accursed! You will be devoured by ghosts!"

"You'll stay!" Shaffeck handed the package the native had carried to Chemile. "I guess this is what you've been waiting for."

The package contained four others, recordings addressed to various officers. Luden pursed his lips as he read the labels.

"Three barracks and the core inspection plant. That ties in with the distribution of the other recordings. If they should vanish the operation would be ended in more ways than one."

"Time's getting short, Jarl," reminded Chemile. He glanced at the sky; the dark orb was at the edge of its bright twin. "We've still got to synchronize the new recordings."

It was a painstaking business of small adjustments and delicate manipulations. The recordings varied a trifle, both in weight and size; it was unimportant for normal playing, but enough to cause one to lag a microsecond after the other when tripped in unison. Chemile sweated as he worked, the pickup heads unactivated, only the feeds of the three players operational.

Luden remained calm.

"We have time, Veem. Only when the white sun is fully eclipsed can we hope to succeed. Now adjust the tension of number two player. Right. Stand by for test."

He pressed a button on the control panel, watching as

three lamps winked, a synchronizing unit giving the variation.

"Number one is lagging, Veem."

. . . Another adjustment, another, more. By the time Luden was satisfied it was time to move.

The *Mordain* rose in the eerie gloom, Chemile at the controls, Luden in the laboratory facing his instruments, monitoring panels, some new ones which he had devised to measure the direction and intensity of the transdimensional forces.

The ground streamed past below, oddly mottled with strange configurations, hills seeming to vanish, to be replaced by massed trees, a thing which lifted a transparent head and opened wide gaping jaws.

Scene was overlaid on scene, the two worlds now very close in vibrational phase. Matter from one needed only a relatively slight stimulus to cross from one to the other.

"Jarl, we're nearing the city." Chemile's voice was tense over the speaker. "Altitude?"

"Fifty feet, Veem." Luden checked his instruments. "Move a little to the south. Right. Now to the east. Hold!"

He frowned at the wavering patch of brightness on one of the screens. Needles on the panels rose from their pins, wavering, some falling as others rose.

"We are wrongly positioned, Veem. Drop to twenty feet. . . . That's better."

"Not if we have to move fast, Jarl. And there could be a hill or something on the other side. Can't we go higher?"

"Perhaps. There could be another focal point of emission from the nexus. We have time to search for it. Rise directly from this point."

The wavering patch of brightness dimmed, almost vanished, then returned with flaring intensity.

"Hold, Veem! Altitude?"

"Five hundred feet. There's a slight wind; you want me to compensate?"

"Yes. It is essential that we maintain this position."

Luden rested his finger on a button, his eyes on the swinging hand of a chronometer. "I am going to activate the players in three seconds. Mark! Two! Three!"

Sound began to whisper through the *Mordain:* the tintinnabulation of bells, the pulse of drums, the thin, high ringing of beaten metal. The sounds swelled, growing, sympathetic vibrations whispering from the bulkheads and the hull.

The volume had been set high, the players fed with all the power they could safely take. As the noise rose Luden muffled his ears, his eyes bright as he watched the instruments.

At the controls Chemile gritted his teeth, feeling his bones begin to ache and his nerves to twitch. His eyes narrowed as he kept the *Mordain* in position with deft hands.

The ground below seemed to roil as if from an unseen earthquake, twisting like the scum on the surface of boiling water. There was a montage of trees, then a building, bare rock, sand, trees again, strange figures which rose to vanish, winged shapes with peculiar heads, something like a squatting idol, the glimmer of a sea.

And then came a pulse, an expanding shock wave which hit him, passed through him, the controls, the hull itself.

And the ground below became clear and firm.

It was strange ground with a strange building and little shapes running and falling. Chemile could pick out the figures of men and the eye-bright shafts of stabbing energy which reached toward them.

"Jarl!" Veem's voice rang through the silence. "It's Cap and he's in trouble!"

Chapter Fourteen

They had attacked when the last band of light had left the sky, creeping forward in the brooding stillness, natural shadows thickened by the eclipse, the forbidding jungle darkness.

It was a time of terror when the natives huddled in their huts and those who had agreed to help began to change their minds.

Kennedy heard a mutter, a curse, the smack of a fist against flesh. Ormond loomed beside him, rubbing the knuckles of his right hand.

"Another would-be deserter, Cap," he said grimly. "I caught him just in time."

"His weapons?"

"He had a Dione. I've given it to one of the others." He turned, squinting into the darkness. "If it hadn't been for that curse you laid on them we would have lost them all by now."

The threat had been spoken with much mumbo jumbo, emphasized by the ceremonial shedding of blood, a bit of primitive magic which Kennedy had invented to instill obedience in the native warriors. The blood had been collected from a minor cut on the arm and hidden. Kennedy's curse was that if the natives ran or showed fear, then their blood would be fed to the ghosts and they would follow it.

So far, aside from a few whose panic had overwhelmed their terror, it had worked.

"We've got to press on," said Kennedy. "Get them to the building before they break."

It rose before them, glowing in the darkness, green fire tracing the columns, the fringe of the dome roof. The area around it was deserted, but Kennedy knew that men would be watching—the blank-faced, robot-like guards of Kaifeng. Those men knew no fear; they would fight and die, killing as they died in obedience to their master.

Crouched in the scrub at the edge of the cleared area, Kennedy examined the target. One of the arches facing him held an open door. It was inviting, but it could be a trap. Others, closed, could shield waiting men. The area itself could be laced with electronic beams, tell-tales that would signal their approach to those in the operations room.

And yet they had to take the building and destroy the machine it contained. They would get back to a familiar world if they could or close the portal if they couldn't. But above all they had to kill Kaifeng.

"It looks tough, Cap." Ormond had evaluated the situation with a trained eye. "Direct assault or split our forces?"

"Split." Separating the men would lower the odds against picking an unlucky point. "You take the right, Penza, you take the left. Deploy. I'll go in and try to make a breach. If I fail, make a concerted effort from opposed sides. If I make it, one group follow at a time to back me up, the other giving covering fire. Once inside split and fan out. When we clear the lower level we can join up to continue the attack."

He waited as rustling sounds came from either side, men moving into position, reluctant natives goaded on by a sprinkle of trained men. A shadow at his side, a corporal, drew in his breath as he checked his Dione.

"If I don't make it, Cap—"

"You'll make it!" Kennedy was harsh. This was no time for doubt. "Just keep moving and firing. Ready? Let's go!"

Like a shadow Kennedy loped from the vegetation, heading at a zigzagging run to a closed door. The corporal stayed close at his heels. The natives could no longer restrain their impulse to shout.

"The stupid idiots! They—"

The corporal died as fire blasted from the building, the shaft of energy searing his heart, his lungs. Kennedy dropped, rolling, firing as he rolled. Flame and smoke burst from the closed door; a sprom cannon began to sew the area with craters from an upper level.

"Cap!" Saratov's voice was a roar. "Back! Back!"

Retreat was impossible. Kennedy rose and lunged forward, feeling the greenly illuminated wall of the building at his shoulder. Ormond was advancing from one side, Saratov from another; in seconds the air was a mass of flames, shouts, screams, the rolling explosions of missiles, the ululating cries of the terrified natives as they ran away.

They fell quickly in pools of blood, arms, legs, internal organs spattered by the whining hail of death.

But, dying, they saved the others.

Ormond sank to the ground, panting, blood running from a lacerated scalp. Kennedy, his face burned by a near miss, stared grimly at the debacle. Saratov, nursing a wounded arm, grunted as he fired.

"A washout, Cap. If those natives hadn't yelled we would have stood a chance."

"We still have one." Kennedy lowered the Dione, the barrel hot with repeated firing. "You maintain fire from here. I'll go around and try to sneak in from the other side."

"Across that open ground?" Ormond shook his head. "Cap, you'd never stand a chance!"

"One man might."

"It took a miracle to get us back to the jungle, Cap. It won't happen twice." Saratov was emphatic. "I'm not going to let you kill yourself. Maybe later we—" He broke off, looking at the sky. "Cap! It's the *Mordain!*"

It came from the sky like a thunderbolt, guns firing, blotches appearing on the walls of the building, flame pouring out as the heavy-duty Dione in the turret blasted a torrent of energy. It landed with a shower of dirt from beneath the hull, cutting a wide furrow in the ground. Small trees crashed as it halted in the vegetation. As it came to rest, its bulk a shield from the gunners in the building, a port fell open.

"Up and in!" snapped Kennedy. "Quickly, all of you! Make sure you get all the wounded!"

Luden stood in the lock. He said urgently, "We haven't much time, Cap. If we hope to return we have to establish the counter-field within a few minutes. Otherwise we must remain until the next darktime."

"We'll make it, Jarl." Kennedy turned, called into the darkness. "Penza?"

"Here, Cap!" The giant appeared carrying a man over each shoulder. The wounded men groaned as he set them down.

"Get to the engines. Full protective field. Ormond! Hurry up with those men!"

"I've got them." The officer entered the lock. "I'll check and let you know when we're all aboard."

Chemile was at the controls maintaining the fire of the guns, washes of blistering energy dimming the emerald glow of the building. As Kennedy dropped into the turret-seat, Chemile said over the speakers, "Yours, Cap. Right?"

"Right!"

Kennedy gripped the releases. Through the sights he could see a group of men running from the building carrying a large-caliber torp projector, a missile which would blow a hole in the *Mordain*. A touch and the big Dione swung to embrace them in flame.

But where there had been one there could be more, and the vessel was a sitting duck.

"Ormond! Loaded yet?"

"Loaded, Cap!"

"Seal hull. Veem, let's move!"

Air whined about the hull as the ship lifted just in time. A tremendous gout of fire rose from where it had rested, the blue-white glare of an atomic missile fired from the roof of the building. From turrets, large-caliber multiple sprom cannon filled the air with a hail of missiles, the screens flaring as they struck, the hull ringing to the impact of explosions. Speed alone saved them, the building falling behind and below as Chemile took evasive action.

"That building, Cap." Luden was incredulous. "I saw it as we landed, the Zheltyana Seal."

"Yes, Jarl."

"Imagine what it means? A working artifact constructed by the Ancient Race. They must have built it to save this world."

"It is possible," admitted Kennedy. "Kaifeng thought so. A pity we have to destroy it."

"But, Cap—"

"Destroy it," said Kennedy flatly. "You know why, Jarl. We don't dare leave it intact. Kaifeng or others like him might want to use it." His voice deepened, became harsh. "Kaifeng!"

His ship could be close. If it was, the battle was far from over. Kennedy scanned the area as Chemile swept the *Mordain* in a wide, flat curve, seeing nothing but the empty air, the ground below.

"Cap!" Luden's voice held strain and Kennedy could guess at the reason. Neither of them liked to destroy, but now they had no choice. Even so, Luden couldn't pretend to enjoy it. "We are running out of time. The counter-field must be established and we have to regain the exact point of entry."

"Which was?"

"Approximately five hundred feet over the nexus, Cap, the building. It will take a few minutes for the transfer to be completed."

But those would be minutes in which they would hang suspended, Kennedy knew, an easy target for the guns below.

"Is the nexus important to the transfer, Jarl?"

"I don't know, Cap. Logically it is essential. The forces contained in the building provide a field to augment the natural space-tension produced by the eclipse. I assume that when you talk of destroying the nexus you are referring to delayed-action torpedoes."

It was the logical method, but it couldn't be used.

Kennedy said, "Before we can establish the return we have to knock out those guns. While we're at it we may as well finish the job. Check your figures. Veem, make some sweeps close to the building. I want to scare the hell out of any natives who might be around."

Kennedy tensed at the guns as Chemile sent the *Mordain* as directed. Flames rose before the nose of the vessel, dirt torn and sent flying by the hammering impact of shells from the multiple sprom cannon.

A blast of fire erupted from the building, a torpedo which missed and exploded far to one side in the jungle, then came missiles. The ship veered, jerking in the tormented air, the blast of impact echoing through the hull.

"Damage?"

"Lower compartment holed in the left quadrant," reported Luden.

"Penza?"

"Sealed and firm, Cap. But the screens can't hold in atmosphere. We're losing too much power through leakage."

Time was passing, seconds running into minutes; the natives had received all the warning he could give.

Kennedy snapped, "Up, Veem. I'm going to use torps. Jarl, get ready to use that field." His hands were busy as he spoke, priming the atomic torpedoes which rested in their bays. He set the fuses for a two-second delay, time enough for them to escape the man-made holocaust which would shortly flower below.

"Right, Veem. Now!"

The *Mordain* turned, leveled, dipped to the glowing building far beneath. Kennedy aligned it in his sights, seeing the domed roof, the enigmatic fringe, the massed weapons toward the center. For a moment he studied it as it grew, then, regretfully, he pressed the releases.

Slender shapes flashed from the launching tubes, the torpedoes lancing like arrows to hit, to penetrate, to bury themselves deep.

"Up!"

The explosion came as they raced for safety, a vivid, blue-white glare which rose to brighten the night with a new sun. Air blasted from the point of impact, a gusting storm which caught the *Mordain* and drew it, tumbling and turning, stabilizers whining as Chemile fought to maintain control.

And, where the building had stood, there was nothing —nothing but a wide crater, glowing redly in the gloom, a scooped-out hole which had contained the nexus and the threat.

"Cap!" Luden was tense. "I'm trying to establish the counter-field now. Hold, Veem. Mark!"

The vessel sang.

It pulsed with a mounting vibration which reached and passed the limits of audibility, causing metal to quiver. It hummed in a rising shrill, hanging as if poised while eardrums threatened to burst, as bones ached and glass shattered. The noise reached a crescendo, then fell into an abrupt silence.

"Cap!" Luden turned as Kennedy entered the laboratory. "We needed the nexus. I don't know if we can pass over with the extra mass we're carrying. If the balance should tip the other way . . ."

. . . They would be stranded, Kennedy knew, lost in a world from which they could never escape now that the building had been destroyed. They would be living ghosts to haunt the darktime of Epidoris.

"Is there anything we can do, Jarl?"

"Nothing, Cap," said Luden dully. "Nothing but wait."

Suspended between two planes of existence, poised on a razor's edge while seconds dragged slowly, they had time for thought, for memories.

. . . Of black hair and violet eyes, a voice that held the chime of bells, a girl who had subconsciously given him his life.

Then Kennedy felt the *Mordain* jerk a little, moving in some other dimension than the three of normal space. It seemed to slip, then steady while blurs on the screen took on form and substance.

"Cap!" Chemile's voice was triumphant. "Jarl! We made it!"

Kennedy said nothing, looking at the screens and the scene below, the shapes of houses and the distant tower of the installation.

DAW BOOKS

The saga of Grainger of the Hooded Swan

DAWsf
BOOKS

☐ **UNDER THE GREEN STAR by Lin Carter.** A marvel adventure in the grand tradition of Burroughs and Merritt.
(#UQ1030—95¢)

☐ **WHEN THE GREEN STAR CALLS by Lin Carter.** Beyond Mars shines the beacon of exotic adventure. A sequel by popular demand!
(#UQ1062—95¢)

☐ **BY THE LIGHT OF THE GREEN STAR by Lin Carter.** The unforgettable third novel of this marvel saga.
(#UQ1120—95¢)

☐ **HERE ABIDE MONSTERS by Andre Norton.** That parallel world was just off the map and out of legendry.
(#UY1134—$1.25)

☐ **HUNTERS OF GOR by John Norman.** The eighth novel of the fabulous saga of Tari Cabot on Earth's orbital twin.
(#UW1102—$1.50)

☐ **THE SPELL SWORD: A DARKOVER NOVEL by Marion Zimmer Bradley.** The latest in this wonder world series.
(#UQ1131—95¢)

DAW BOOKS are represented by the publishers of Signet and Mentor Books, THE NEW AMERICAN LIBRARY, INC.

THE NEW AMERICAN LIBRARY, INC.,
P.O. Box 999, Bergenfield, New Jersey 07621

Please send me the DAW BOOKS I have checked above. I am enclosing
$_____(check or money order—no currency or C.O.D.'s).
Please include the list price plus 25¢ a copy to cover mailing costs.

Name_____

Address_____

City_____State_____Zip Code_____
Please allow at least 3 weeks for delivery